River of Porcupines

RIVER OF PORCUPINES

G. K. AALBORG

FIVE STAR
A part of Gale, a Cengage Company

GALE
A Cengage Company

Farmington Hills, Mich • San Francisco • New York • Waterville, Maine
Meriden, Conn • Mason, Ohio • Chicago

Copyright © 2018 by Gordon Aalborg
Five Star Publishing, a part of Gale, a Cengage Company

LIBRARY OF CONGRESS CATALOGING-IN-PUBLICATION DATA

Names: Aalborg, Gordon, author.
Title: River of porcupines / G.K. Aalborg.
Description: First edition. | Farmington Hills, Mich. : Five Star, a part of Gale, Cengage Learning, [2018]
Identifiers: LCCN 2018014288 (print) | LCCN 2018016648 (ebook) | ISBN 9781432838126 (ebook) | ISBN 9781432838119 (ebook) | ISBN 9781432838157 (hardcover)
Subjects: | GSAFD: Romantic suspense fiction. | Western stories.

Classification: LCC PR9619.3.A22 (ebook) | LCC PR9619.3.A22 R58 2018 (print) | DDC 823/.914—dc23
LC record available at https://lccn.loc.gov/2018014288

First Edition. First Printing: November 2018
Find us on Facebook—https://www.facebook.com/FiveStarCengage
Visit our website—http://www.gale.cengage.com/fivestar/
Contact Five Star Publishing at FiveStar@cengage.com

Printed in Mexico
1 2 3 4 5 6 7 22 21 20 19 18

For Dana—who was there at the beginning of this novel . . .
And for Deni—who was there at the end.

ACKNOWLEDGMENTS

I would be remiss if I didn't acknowledge the invaluable assistance given by my wonderful editor, Hazel Rumney. She is the type and quality of editor I want to be when I grow up . . . and I've had any number during a long career to allow comparisons.

Thank you, Hazel. It has been a privilege working with you, and learning.

CHAPTER ONE

Spring came to the Kootenay Plains in a blinding swirl of wind-lashed rain and hail. It drove the gaunt Blackfoot ponies to shelter in the pine thickets and their owners to huddle coughing in the winter-thickened stench of their lodges.

A few of the braver Indians, with cautious glances at the shattering sky, took blankets to their favored buffalo ponies, but most cowered before the anger of the storm, terrified by Nature's sudden mood change.

No blanket was brought to the shaggy young white man chained to a tree at the edge of the camp, nearly naked and with no protection from the storm. He also looked to the sky, but Garth Cameron had no fear of the lightning serpents; he was surprised and thankful merely to be alive, and whether death came from God's lance or that of an Indian wouldn't make much difference.

The antics of his captors both amused and enraged him, and he lunged to the limits of the thirty-foot chain around his naked waist, roaring with abusive laughter. He combined the few contemptuous Blackfoot words he knew with an extensive vocabulary of English, French, and Gaelic obscenities in a barrage that would have brought him applause from his companions at Rocky Mountain House.

The sodden, scurrying Indians ignored him.

"Lousy, stinking varmints," he muttered, shaking his huge fists. "Ah, well, at least I can get clean, long's I don't freeze in

9

the process."

He retreated to the dubious shelter of the tall jack pine to which his chain was riven with a massive, rusty spike, then stripped off what remained of his buckskin breeches and threw them to the tiny remaining bit of grass that had survived his four months of pacing. It might have been nice, he considered, to have a handy anthill so he could remove at least some of the vermin that infested his tattered clothing and winter-grown hair and bedraggled, reddish beard.

At one point he had believed the vermin might carry him off chain and all; now he was beyond any concerns about modesty or a few louse bites. Water streaming over his winter-white body, he bent to slip off his moccasins, the once beautifully-beaded remembrance of a brief dalliance with the daughter of a rum-craving Cree sub-chief. After throwing them, too, to the cleansing rain and hail, along with the scabrous buffalo robe that was his only other protection from the weather, he moved around and around within the limits of his chain, trying to stay warm.

He'd often thought his anger at himself should have been enough to warm him. He was a damned fool and worse and would doubtless be told so at length if he ever returned to Rocky Mountain House.

It had been a childish desire to mark his twenty-first birthday as he had the several before it—with feminine company—that had landed him at the end of this Blackfoot slave chain, and it was little satisfaction that he would never forget it . . . not now.

Older and wiser members of David Thompson's trading party had many times warned him against slipping off to the bushes with tasty young squaws while their fathers or husbands were being supplied with cheap trade rum to separate them from their furs.

"One of these days, some big chief he's going to make a *capon* out of you. Then maybe you will listen," little René

Giroux had cautioned during one of the wizened voyageur's infrequent moments of seriousness. Garth had laughed; it was like getting culinary advice from a wolverine.

It was said of René that he had the mind of a horse trader, the strength of an ox, and the instincts of a rutting bull elk. He'd been forty years on the rivers and had left Métis children among every tribe from Montreal to the shining Rockies.

Even David Thompson, who frequently spent more time doodling with his maps than worrying about the habits of his men—or, more important, the competition from the Hudson's Bay Company at neighboring Acton House—also had mentioned the matter to young Garth Cameron. But it was a waste of words; Garth was already fully into the pattern described by his cohorts as "a short life but a merry one . . . if you keep your hair." And he was enjoying every day of it along with many of the nights.

A full six-foot-four in his moccasins, he was still reaching for the 260 pounds that would someday grace his massive frame. Whether the occasion called for heaving up a 400-pound pack, carrying a canoe that most men couldn't handle as a pair, or chasing a succulent young squaw, he considered himself fully able and even more willing. A gaunt and gangling youth of sixteen when he'd made his first trip to the mountains, he was counted a man grown by the brawling, hard-slaving voyageurs before they'd reached the forks of the Saskatchewan. His red-gold hair and beard had earned him the pet name of Sun Buffalo beneath many a native trade blanket during his trips west, and fear talk from the monkey-like René or his sober patron had been ignored by Garth. At least until this incident.

He had been lying in the slender arms of Meadowlark, the third and obviously little-used wife of old Three Bears of the mountain Blackfoot, when the old warrior and two of his sons—both substantially older than Meadowlark—disrupted the scene.

Believing the old sub-chief and his headmen were out of commission after liberal draughts of trade rum, Garth had enticed the girl into walking with him to a dense pine thicket upstream from the post. She hadn't understood most of what he said, but the throbbing bulge at his groin needed little interpretation. Within minutes, they were snugly ensconced on a soft bed of pine needles, and all need for words was past.

His passions temporarily drained, Garth had been idly toying with the girl's young breasts when a whistling war club exploded something in his head. He'd awakened to the jarring trot of a scrawny pony whose greatest desire and accomplishment seemed to involve stumbling over its own feet to the discomfort of its unwilling passenger.

Twisting his throbbing head, Garth had been able to see the hunched and welted back of Meadowlark on the pony ahead. She had been beaten until her back was a blood-sodden mess of tattered flesh and buckskin.

The sight stirred young Garth to rage, and despite his head wound he began to struggle against the rawhide thongs that bound him hand-to-foot beneath the pony's belly. A futile gesture; one of the young Blackfoot outriders reined up long enough to smack Garth across the head a second time, and he didn't stir again, even when the Indians stopped for the night and he was brutally kicked from the pony's back into a convenient snow bank.

Hunger and thirst were gnawing fires in his gut when Garth woke the next time. Lying quietly, bound so securely he had little other choice, he watched through half-closed eyes as his captors settled into a temporary camp at the mouth of a stream he thought was probably the Ram River, for all the good that knowledge might do him.

The chief's eldest son, Walking Dog, noticed Garth's return to consciousness and strode over to where the captive was trying to sit upright. Garth was still trying to remember his rudimentary Blackfoot vocabulary when Walking Dog paused before him, spat in his face, then kicked him in the mouth. The kick slammed Garth back into the bole of a tree, blood frothing from his crushed lips to feed the anger rising to growls in his throat.

He struggled against his bonds as the chief's son strode back to the central fire, thumbing an obscene gesture over his shoulder and laughing to his fellows. Meadowlark also received her share of kicking, but Garth was ignored until the Indians had finished their evening meal. Then Walking Dog returned, carrying a bowl of stinking gruel into which he shoved Garth's face until suffocation seemed not only imminent but preferable.

The savages laughed as Garth was repeatedly half-drowned in the slop while being forced to eat like a dog. The old man, especially, seemed to enjoy the sport, although his nearly toothless grin seemed less one of enjoyment than of anticipation. The crude gestures that accompanied his harsh, guttural commentary, and the cruel satisfaction the band seemed to take in tormenting Meadowlark, made it obvious Garth had suffering yet to come.

He had heard, as had all voyageurs, of "Baldy" St. Jean, who'd been castrated and scalped—but, significantly, allowed to survive—after being caught diddling a Cree woman near Paint Creek House on the Vermilion.

St. Jean's companions had found him the next day, hogtied and unconscious in a pool of his own blood outside the gates of the stockade. The flirtatious squaw had coyly eyed him again some months later when her band returned for more trade, but his mind was going by then, and he had returned her sly glances with blank stares. Later that winter, he had fled screaming from the encampment one night and fallen, in his erratic flight, through a hole in the lifting ice.

Visions of such a fate, combined with Garth's injuries, brought the vile stew spewing from his stomach, to the pleasure of his greasy captors. Walking Dog strutted over to kick him once more, and then the entire band rolled into their robes, leaving Garth as he had fallen.

It was more than an hour before he managed to squirm into the carpet of pine needles and gain a measure of protection against the quickening wind and blowing snow. Sleep was impossible; he spent that first night alternating between fitful, shivering naps and painful waking spells in which he could not escape the stinging cold. By morning there was six inches of fresh snow and Garth was kicked awake by Walking Dog and made to grovel into another bowl of stinking gruel, but the band was clearly in a hurry. Garth was slung hastily across the harsh-ribbed spine of another pony, and they were back on the trail by full light.

A week later, they reached the tribal wintering grounds on the Kootenay Plains, where Garth was dumped from his pony and chained to the jack pine where he would become the winter's entertainment for at least some of the Blackfoot.

Not that he had to provide much, nor was much provided for him. Full winter arrived the next day, and Garth was often as not ignored in the band's simple struggle for survival. An aged squaw occasionally fed him while taunting him about Meadowlark's sufferings, which apparently were worse than his own, and he was thrown the mangy buffalo robe to protect him from freezing to death. But at least the torments from Walking Dog and his father were limited to the occasional passing kick.

The children and camp dogs spent a few days teasing him, but the children soon tired of the game and the dogs quickly learned the lessons he taught them via vicious kicks and sweeps of slackened chain. By the night of the lightning storm, there wasn't a dog left in camp, anyway; during the final months of that harsh winter they had contributed heavily to the thin soup in the camp cooking pots.

Garth also had suffered. By pulling boughs from the jack pine and arranging the mangy buffalo robe, he'd managed to avoid freezing. But the lack of sufficient food and the inactivity had taken their toll. Stripped now of his tattered buckskins, he looked in worse condition than the gaunt native ponies. The massiveness of his frame was accentuated by his lack of flesh, and rib bones threatened to puncture his frost-burned and louse-ridden hide.

The ground inside the circle of his chain was paced to mush, which the driving rain was now splattering upon what remained of his clothes. So Garth wrung the water from them and put them on again. The old robe he beat against the tree trunk, then draped over a low branch in hopes the rain might drive off or wash off the remaining vermin.

Squatting against the tree, he shivered with the chill and idly conjectured if the storm would mean another day without food. Many such days had spent themselves during his captivity, and with meat so scarce during the past month in particular, the little he'd been given was enough to maintain life, but only a semblance of his old strength and endurance.

He ended up, as usual, sitting up for most of the night beneath the mountain jack pine while his thoughts raced with the forks of the sky-serpent lightning around him. Spring was here—or near as, damn it! Soon the ponies would begin to fatten on the new grass, and his Indian captors would be moving on . . . but to where? And would he live to see their summering grounds among the buffalo?

The main Blackfoot bands, he knew, ranged throughout the prairie country of the buffalo, down along the Red Deer and the Bow Rivers, out along the mighty forked Saskatchewan. But where the North Saskatchewan swung further north below

Rocky Mountain House, the tribes and the trade changed with it. Blackfoot tribesmen still traded at the posts of Quagmire Hall, Forts Edmonton and Augustus, and the island post of Fort de L'Isle, but the furs of the northern Cree were finding their way in growing numbers into the hands of the North-West Company. The older Hudson's Bay Company continually moved further into the wilderness in attempts to thwart the "pedlars," while Alexander Mackenzie and his much younger XY Company proved a nuisance to both major trading companies.

The chill grew, and Garth Cameron shrugged closer into the soaking buffalo robe, gradually drifting into a fitful doze that was punctuated by the spears and arrows of lightning in the darkening mountain sky.

He was alive tonight, he thought, and would manage somehow to be the same tomorrow. What he needed was food and some luck.

CHAPTER TWO

The Blackfoot later called it "the place where the sky kills," and never again would they pitch their buffalo-hide lodges within a mile of there. Three times, the spears of lightning stabbed into the camp of old Three Bears, and within moments the band was leaderless and four people fewer in number.

The aging chief was first. When the first lightning bolt smashed into the rocks of his fire-pit, he dived headlong through the teepee flap into a second crackling lance that split him from scalp lock to moccasins. On the other side of the encampment, the widow Moose Calf Crying and her two small children died seconds later, when their lodge was savaged by the lightning, leaving only the fire stones and three charred bodies to the hammers of the rain.

Garth's tree became a gargantuan torch from yet another assault by the lightning gods, and when Walking Dog slunk from his teepee to look about the storm-lashed camp, he saw clearly the body of his prisoner sprawled beneath the flare. Drawn by the screams from his father's lodge, he stepped over the patriarch's remains, clubbed Meadowlark and her two senior wives until they ceased their wailing, then ordered them to begin the requisite funeral preparations while he tried to restore order to what would now be his inheritance.

The camp was in chaos. Women and children were hopping about like screaming grasshoppers, and most of the men were engaged in trying to calm the thrashing, nervous ponies tied inside the circle of lodges. Walking Dog's own prized buffalo hunter was tethered near the blazing tree, but as he rushed to calm it, he gave no thought to his captive.

He was severing the pony's rawhide tether when Garth smashed his skull like a melon with a slackened loop of rusty chain. Then Garth sank to his knees in the mud, exhausted from swinging the ten-foot length of warm iron links.

It took all his concentration to struggle to his feet, pick up the fallen knife, and begin whispering calm into the skittish horse. Alarmed at the rich odor of blood and brains from its dead owner, the pony reared to the end of the tether, but once Garth got his hands on it, the animal quieted enough that he could lead it from the thicket and out onto the steep river trail.

The lightning that had cut Garth's chain had knocked him senseless, and the heat scurrying up the old iron had left a searing burn where the chain touched his waist. The driving rain had revived him and enabled him to slink into cover in the spruce thicket near where the horses sheltered. He had been trying to sneak up on the closely tethered ponies when Walking Dog arrived, and the sight of his tormentor left Garth without a moment's thought of future caution. But, calmed now, and wary of pursuit despite its unlikelihood, he eased up on the horse's back and walked it down the slippery path, cautious and watchful for other Indians he expected would soon be out rounding up scattered ponies.

"Softly now, horse," he murmured at the nervous buffalo pony, thankful with hindsight that it had not turned out to be war-trained. That happenstance could have left him trampled in the mud for daring to touch the animal.

"Now we've got this far, I don't plan to be taken again, so you and I are going to slide out of here slick as a beaver's tit, provided I can find the way."

Like most voyageurs and mountain men of his time, Garth

had listened well to travel tales of canoe and campfire. There were few reliable maps, excepting those of his patron and leader, David Thompson, and all a man could learn of the country by listening was certain to be of value sometime or another. This was one of them.

He'd never been this far up the Saskatchewan, but others had, and his mind was recalling the trails and landmarks of which he'd been told. If he could avoid any horse-chasing members of the camp he had left, there was every chance he could gain a day or even two before serious pursuit might eventuate. Thoroughly demoralized by the storm and the loss of their leaders, it could be a while before anyone noticed he had escaped, and in any event, it would take them time to regroup and plan. With the best of luck, nobody left in the camp would care enough to bother chasing him.

Regardless, it was little use to follow the river too closely; most of the fords governing tributary streams wouldn't be usable with the ice still going out higher in the mountains, and the river was as much a barrier to him now as the mountains themselves.

"Choices," he muttered, gripping the chain to keep it from clinking as he guided the buffalo horse up the first trail he reached that led away from the river, trying to remember any landmarks that might guide him.

The rain fell more softly, but steadily enough to help wash out his trail, so Garth moved along for two days and nights without daring to stop. As the pony reached the higher ground away from the river, it slipped into the smooth mountain walk of a true high-country horse, and Garth was often lulled into semi-consciousness as he slumped over its withers. He barely noticed when the animal turned up a narrow track along the Bighorn, but came sharply awake when the horse literally skidded to a stop where the trail entered a ford near Crescent Falls.

Usually the ford, known to Garth only by reputation, was low enough that a horse would barely wet its hocks. But the early and heavy rains had swollen the Bighorn into a torrent that the pony refused to enter, and Garth was in no shape to argue or doubt its judgment.

With the coming dawn streaking the rain in the eastern sky, he did the only thing he could do. Careful not to release the halter rope, he slipped off the pony's withers and scouted the rock face until he found a fist-sized piece of flint. Then he turned away from the surging waters and, dragging the horse behind him, sought a safe place to hide. A half-mile back from the stream brought him into a tiny, secluded meadow where he could picket the pony, but almost as important was the finding that one edge of the little glade ran down into a thick copse of spruce, providing both fuel and food for a man of Garth's experience and desperate need.

A flock of spruce grouse, foolish as all of their kind, were easy prey to a lengthy pole swung by a starving man. They had been huddled along a low branch in the thicket when Garth first slunk, then rushed in to swing the long stick and knock several of the birds sprawling in a welter of broken necks and wings. Food! And with the chunk of flint and the cheap trade knife for a steel, he could create fire on which to cook it.

An hour later, his belly full and two birds remaining for supper, he sprawled on a bed of spruce boughs and watched the hobbled pony grazing lazily in the small meadow. Garth had made no attempt to remove the chain from round his waist; the cheap trade knife he'd taken from Walking Dog's body was too weak to spring the ancient lock and he feared breaking the knife. The chain grated on his burned skin, but he took consolation in the proven killing value of the slack end.

He slept the afternoon away, cooked the remaining spruce grouse in the remains of his tiny, almost-smokeless fire, and was asleep again by full dark. At midnight, chilled but refreshed, he caught up the pony and rode again to the ford. It had dropped considerably, but still was frothy enough that he had to beat the pony to force it across. Then, turning more east and parallel to the Saskatchewan but a mile from it, he set out in the direction of Rocky Mountain House.

He crossed the headwaters of Chambers Creek early on the fourth day, having stuck to a habit of riding by moonlight and hiding when the sun rose. Now, having seen only one stray pony and no Indians, he figured to make the post by noon . . . with any luck.

Garth decided to chance riding by daylight, this close to the post and safety, though he was still weak and certainly far from peak alertness. His mind called for a caution his fatigued system couldn't maintain, and he was half-asleep atop the plodding Blackfoot pony when he jerked awake to hear other horses approaching.

Cursing his dulled senses, he had barely yanked the small pony into a concealing alder thicket and dismounted when the first of the oncoming horses rounded a bend in the trail, and he clamped his mount's nostrils shut and urged it further into the brush.

Noticing immediately that the packs on the first pony were those of a white man, he almost stepped out to hail the approaching party, but some inner caution held him, and a moment later he was glad of it.

The first person he saw, riding a tall dark horse behind the pack outfit, was Louis Savard, the immense, half-breed woods boss of the Hudson's Bay Company at Acton House and therefore a sworn enemy of any North West Company employee. Savard was known from Montreal to the mountains as a brawler, and tales of his unnatural cruelty were common at camps all along the rivers of the voyageurs. The man had a natural lust for fighting and brutality, and Garth knew he would like nothing better than to get his hands on a half-starved, unarmed, and virtually defenseless member of a rival trading company. A number of deaths were credited to Savard, most of them involving men from other companies who'd been mauled and beaten in so-called fair fights.

With Savard were his expected companions, the half-breed Cardinal brothers from Onion Lake. Their lean, foxy features were in strong contrast to the beard and bulk of the woods boss, and it was easy to see why, among their own people, they were called, "the weasels who run with the bear."

Garth shuddered involuntarily as they straggled slowly past, sure in the knowledge he'd have been safer amongst the Blackfoot than in the hands of this trio. Thankful they were driving the pack ponies ahead of them, wiping out his own tracks before they could be seen by the riders, he waited a full twenty minutes before again venturing out onto the main trail.

He spent that last, uneventful, fifteen miles to the post speculating about the muskets he'd seen in Savard's packs and could find no pleasant explanation. A certain number of guns found their way into Indian hands through trading, but from the looks of this pack train, Savard was planning to outfit an entire Indian band, and Garth's logic told him it could easily be the band he had escaped from, a guarantee of trouble for every trapper and trader along the upper Saskatchewan.

Rivalry between the trading companies had about reached a peak that past summer, and Garth knew there was little to prohibit Savard from instigating all-out war between the Blackfoot and the Norwesters to the benefit of his own firm. He knew also that James Bird, factor at the Hudson's Bay Company post, would openly decry such measures, but once done, he'd limit Savard's punishment to a tongue-lashing in public and likely a pouch of gold behind the closed doors of Acton House.

Bird was a man who lived by the rules of the fur trade—putting furs before any *non*-profit, humanitarian gestures.

The London-based Hudson's Bay Company directors, faced with open defiance of the ridiculous charter they interpreted as claim to an entire continent, were prepared to take any steps to protect their claim. Violence wasn't openly condoned, but it was seldom questioned after the fact, either.

CHAPTER THREE

Louis Savard's father had arrived in Hell with a mouth full of broken teeth and his genitals jammed in amongst them—courtesy of the son he'd beaten on through most of Louis's fourteen childhood years.

Savard's French sire was a deserter from the 1760 Battle of the Thousand Islands on the upper St. Lawrence River. The battle saw the end of the French and Indian war in which Canada fell to British rule. The fighting Savard Père saw was mostly viewed looking over his shoulder as he fled.

The elder Savard had been a sailor and was a malingerer, a coward, and a bully, but a good-looking charmer when he needed to be. He was taken in, hidden, and cared for by Savard's mother, a Caughnawaga Mohawk. He repaid her kindness by routinely beating her and the children he inflicted upon her.

Savard, as large as his father at fourteen, took more than his share of beatings in attempts to divert attention from the other children but reached his breaking point when he caught his sire—drunk as usual—about to molest Savard's older sister Francine, whom he adored. It was the first such incident, to his knowledge, and he knew he had to stop it, not least before a pattern could be established.

Ignoring the pain of his own wounds from a disciplinary session a half-hour earlier, the boy fetched an ox-yoke, smashed his parent across the face with it, then used the man's own skinning knife to slash off his testicles and ram them in amongst the shattered teeth before he slashed open the parental beer belly and, finally, his father's throat.

When he'd caught his breath, he kissed Francine on the cheek, murmured a sad, gentle farewell, then held his fifteen-year-old sister at arm's length for the minutes it took to engrain her ebony hair and dark eyes into his memory. He would never see her again, and he sensed that without knowing why.

Savard didn't bother to say good-bye to his mother, who had been battered from a Mohawk princess even prettier than her daughter into a drunken slattern—slave to the brutal lover she'd once saved from the English cannons.

He struck out on his own, working his way west along the rivers as a courier de bois, voyageur, and general roustabout. He joined the HBC at Cumberland House on the Saskatchewan, the London-based company's first inland trading post. Known as Waskahiganihk by the Cree, the post on Pine Island was the gateway to the western rivers and marked the beginning of the intense rivalry between the HBC and the Montréal traders, later to become the North West Company.

Savard was a recognized woods boss and brawler by the time he reached the western extremities of the North Saskatchewan in 1800. Along the line, he'd acquired the Cardinal brothers from Onion Lake, and they followed him like faithful vultures, doing his dirty work and whatever mischief they thought would please him. They both feared and hated him but managed to thrive in the shadow of his strength.

Savard tolerated and sometimes encouraged the half-breed brothers in fomenting trouble between the companies along the rivers of the fur trade. He had secret plans to establish himself as a serious trader in the mountain west and was ever alert to what opportunities might arise.

His loyalty to James Bird at Acton House was one of

convenience, and both men knew it, but, while it suited his own purposes, Savard was an ideal manager of the rough-and-ready voyageurs and woodsmen employed by the HBC.

Savard was notorious for his violence in this land of violence . . . a brawler and a bruiser who revelled in bullying and power politics of the most physical type. He ruled Acton House with his brutality, using fists, knives, or whatever he required to maintain order amongst the employees.

He'd grown to be as good-looking as his father, with wild, curly, soot-black hair and auburn eyes, but he lacked his sire's natural charm, and Savard's looks were mostly hidden by his untamed hair and thick, heavy beard. Without a shirt, he resembled a shambling black bear.

Mostly a loner, although he drank with the others when the opportunity presented, he generally kept to himself, sharing little of his history or his personal thoughts and feelings. Over the years, he had been involved occasionally with Indian women along the rivers, but always they were older women, usually widows, occasionally captives from tribal conflicts. Never was there any emotional current in these casual involvements, but his fault wasn't cruelty. It came from his blunt, simple indifference. They were a convenience; nothing more.

Then he saw Ilona Baptiste for the first time, with her father in the camp of the free traders between Acton House and Rocky Mountain House. The seventeen-year-old Métis maiden looked up at him, but only briefly. Then she looked away without any indication of having noticed him—not an unusual reaction, in Savard's experience with young native women.

Savard could not look away. "Francine," he whispered, the name drawn from his soul in a shuddering gasp. He looked at Ilona, but his mind and heart saw his sister Francine as clearly as she'd appeared to him those many years before. Only . . . different. Provocative, alluring, fascinating . . . but . . . Every time he saw Ilona—and he made it a point to see her whenever he could—he found himself adrift in an aimless and turbulent sea of emotions he'd nearly forgotten and couldn't really understand. He was drawn by her innocence, but there was an incestuous flavor to the attraction, though he couldn't explain it even to himself. He vowed to have her, but inside him was a romantic notion that she would come to him willingly, freely. It was, he determined, their destiny, and Savard was sufficiently Indian in his soul to be hopelessly superstitious.

Her father's potential influence amongst the Peigan, which made sense to him, added to her allure, as it complemented his own half-formed plans to strike out on his own as a free trader. He'd come west on the rivers, but in his dreams, Savard was a plains Indian, a horseman, a warrior, a leader. One of the highlights of his life had come from joining a band of Indians along the Saskatchewan in the thrill of their mid-summer buffalo hunt.

His interest in Ilona grew throughout the long, boring months of winter in the foothills of the Rocky Mountains, but he never approached her, never spoke to her directly. He discovered her father's debt to the Bay, made a roundabout approach to James Bird, the factor, about paying off the debt, but couldn't close the deal because he couldn't find the words to answer Bird's first question—"Why?"

His own inner confusion annoyed Savard, which made him angry, frustrated, striking out in all directions with strong words and stronger fists.

It fared no better when he approached Ilona's father with a proposal so contrived as to be nonsensical. Perhaps because he more than half expected it, he could almost *see* the scorn on the face of old Jean-Paul Baptiste when Savard offered to pay off his debt. It was as if the old free trapper couldn't determine if Savard was trying to buy his daughter, or sell him a trap line, or . . . ? Savard had reckoned without considering the fierce pride and independence of Baptiste and realized it too late.

"*Je ne comprend pas,*" the old man insisted, then retreated into the stoicism of his native ancestry. It was, to Savard, like attempting to converse with a stone.

The chance to trek south with contraband muskets for the Blackfeet who'd wintered at the Kootenay Plains seemed like an omen offering at least temporary freedom from his frustration.

CHAPTER FOUR

They saw each other at virtually the same moment. The Métis maiden with midnight hair and eyes took one glance at the gaunt, nearly-naked figure on the shambling dun pony and clapped a hand to her mouth as she fled to the relative safety of the free trappers' camp.

With only a brief glance at her facial attractiveness, Garth Cameron watched with interest the movements of her lithe, young body as she ran, then turned the pony in through the gates to Rocky Mountain House and the cries of those who recognized him.

"*Mon Dieu,* you are still alive, you." Small René yanked Garth down from the pony and clasped him in a crushing hug that drove knives through the area of burns at his waist. René looked at the massive chain and the agony on Garth's face, and his broad smile of welcome faded as he quickly released his friend.

"Aiiieee. It is a hard winter you've had, eh? And the chain? You were somebody's pet, maybe? What an ungrateful dog I bet you made. Come now with René; old Pierre will cut off that bear's harness so you can put some food in your thin belly without it hurts too much, eh? By God, you should have stayed away another day or two. Then that chain, it would have fallen right over your hips and saved us the work.

"Where have you been all the winter long, you? Lounging in some chief's lodge while your comrades do all the work? Ha! Grouard . . . tell *le chef* to prepare a feast for our starving young

29

arrival here. And then maybe you had best seek out *le patron* and tell him who is back with us."

He literally dragged Garth to the shed where old Pierre kept his make-shift blacksmithing tools, and within moments the chain was only a rusting memory on the dirt floor.

"That feels fifty pounds lighter," Garth said. "Now, come on, little monkey; let us get me some food and a tot of rum, and I'll tell you all while you see if you can do something about these damned burns."

David Thompson had sent word he would see Garth after the youth was fed and rested, so when they reached the kitchen, Garth slashed a huge chunk off an elk roast sizzling on the spit, had René mix him a tall, hot mug of rum, and settled down to satisfying the cravings of his shrunken stomach.

Considerable rum and two pounds of meat later, he was out cold, and the powerful little voyageur carried him to Garth's own cabin to rest. He dumped Garth on the bunk, stripped off what remained of his clothing, then gently bathed the younger man's body before smearing fresh bear grease on the burns.

"The hair, it will have to wait," he muttered, dolefully shaking his head at the ravages inflicted by vermin and exposure. Then, having done all he could for the moment, he threw a couple of blankets over his young friend and stepped quietly away.

Garth's dreams were chaotic, switching from the brute ugliness of Savard, chasing him naked with an iron whip, to stirring visions of the native girl he'd seen outside the compound. When the rasping voice of René woke him, he rose with a start to find the small voyageur and David Thompson, *le patron*, standing beside the bed.

"Well, young man, you must have quite a tale to tell. Suppose you start at the beginning, since we already know the end," said the factor, whose voice was edged with sarcasm enough that

Garth realized the man knew quite sufficient already how and why he had managed to be kidnapped. Humbly, he recounted his adventures while Thompson sat scowling across the table.

Even mention of Savard and his pack train of muskets brought little response from Thompson. He merely grunted and gestured for Garth to continue. The story complete, Thompson rose abruptly from his stool and walked to the door.

"I shall look into this business of Savard and the guns," he said, then turned to René.

"See that the boy gets some decent clothes and a sulfur bath to ease his wounds. Cameron, you take a few days to rest up, and then it's back to work. But take it easy until you've regained your strength. Living as you have, I am surprised you're not rotten with scurvy. We will speak further of this other business later."

Garth caught René's subdued motion to silence and refrained from the comment he'd been about to make. Lying back on the bunk, he waited until Thompson was well away before exploding in a volley of curses.

"What the hell's the matter with the old man, anyway?" he cried. "Here Savard is probably planning to get us all massacred, and *le patron* merely says he will 'look into it.' Doesn't he realize what this could mean to the trade all along the river?"

"Softly, softly now. It does no good, this shouting and making bad noises. *Le patron* is a good man . . . the best. You must be assured he will do what is right. Now wrap up in that blanket and come along, because Pierre has arranged for you a sulfur bath of the greatest vileness, something you sorely need.

"And, while you are soaking, René will find for you some new buckskins. I saw one of Etienne Laflamme's daughters around here a day or so ago. When I tell her for whom I wish these new clothes, you will be dressed like a chief. Now come, to the tub."

It was indeed one of the vilest mineral baths Garth had ever smelled, but when he had been properly scrubbed, and his filthy hair cleaned and rinsed and soaped again with the harsh lye soap he was sure Pierre used on the horses, he believed any vermin problem was solved. Not even the stoutest of Blackfoot fleas or lice could have lived through the old blacksmith's ministrations.

René returned as the bath finished, carrying a pair of brightly beaded moccasins but no other clothes.

"Aha, *mon ami*. Best you save that blanket. It will be at least one day before we can have made for you anything else to wear. Old Etienne's daughter, she is off playing house with one of the Bay's boatmen, so I must get the old grandmother to make for you the clothes. She is not so fast as the girl—and not so pretty, either—but she sews well, and it will be worth the wait.

"In the meantime, you should cover up that most ugly naked-ness and come with me to the kitchen for some good moose-nose stew that our chef has prepared. *Le patron* said we should put upon your bones some meat, before he whips it off for your stupidity. The earlier we begin, the sooner you can get the whip-ping over with, *non*?"

The stew was indeed excellent, and Garth was well into his third helping when the thought of the girl at the gate conjured up visions in his mind.

"René . . . when I rode in . . . there was this girl just outside the gate. She ran into the free trappers' camp. Did you see her? Do you know who she is?"

"Aha. Two good meals and our young friend is ready once again to seek out a fine young cow. Do you never learn, you?" The old voyageur laughed.

"Let me see. There were many girls outside the post then. That fat daughter of Adrian Plouffe . . . but of course it is not her of whom you speak. And then there was that long-nosed one, the squaw that is shacked up with Charonnaise . . . but if I remember, you tried that one on the way up river. It was at Terre Blanche Fort, was it not?"

He laughed at Garth's protestations of innocence then leapt back into his monologue.

"Ah, I know the one you mean. That skinny little Métis chicken with the wealth of hair. Oh, *mon ami* . . . you must stay away from that one. She is claimed by that brute Savard, I think. You mix with that one, and we will have for sure a company war.

"*Oui* . . . that is the one. She is the daughter of the free trapper old Jean-Paul Baptiste. Almost white, she is. Her mother was a quarter-breed Peigan. She came out with her papa only a few months ago, and Savard, he is try to claim her because the old man, he got too sick to pay an old debt with the Bay, so Savard paid it for him, I'm thinking. Or offered to. Baptiste has a strong voice amongst the Peigan, and his influence could be important.

"Savard has not had the girl yet, because James Bird, the factor there, is keeping too close a watch. But he will . . . and soon, you can bet. Stay away from that little *poule,* my friend, or you will disappear again, and we will get you back in little pieces."

Garth was thinking of some brave retort when the door burst open and little Paul, the expedition's clerk, charged in to say the factor wanted to see Garth, "right now!"

With misgivings about the interview but little choice, Garth wrapped himself in the blanket, drained his toddy, and walked to the house of David Thompson. Stooping to enter the low doorway, he nearly lost the blanket, and when he saw the girl sitting inside, he came equally near to losing what remained of his composure.

"Come in, lad . . . come in." The factor's voice was strangely welcoming, hardly the tongue lashing Garth had been expecting. He was further confused by the girl's presence, but when he realized she was too shy to look at him, he ventured to study her while Thompson was speaking.

"I am most concerned about your encounter with Savard and the likelihood he was en route to meet with the Blackfoot, Mr. Cameron. If we can properly interpret what you've seen, it could mean a great deal of trouble for our company and all whites along the river. I am surprised that James Bird has not put a stop to such nonsense, because even his own people will be in danger, but . . .

"This young lady is Ilona Baptiste, old Jean-Paul's girl. Her part in our discussion I shall reveal to you in due course, but be assured it is important.

"Now . . . while you were in that Blackfoot camp—it was old Three Bears' camp, was it not?—did you see anything to indicate the presence of other white men? Any whites not known to you?"

Garth swiftly thought back through his captivity, then had to reply in the negative. The only thing distinctively of *white* origins was the trade knife he'd taken during his escape, and such knives were now common amongst the trading tribes.

Thompson poured out a toddy for Garth and then sat back introspectively, giving Garth further opportunity to inspect the girl. She was, he decided, as close to perfect as a woman could be. Lustrous hair set off a face in which only a trace of Indian ancestry showed. And even this, he decided, added rather than detracted from the whole. Her straight-cut doeskin tunic, halting slightly below the knee, revealed a hint of shapely leg drifting into typical high-cut leggings, and her small feet were in delicately beaded moccasins. The swelling bosom beneath the tunic was sufficient to stir Garth beneath his blanket, and he was shifting awkwardly to disguise that stirring when Thompson resumed his speech.

"I expect orders to move west next spring," he said, speaking slowly as he chose his words. "There is a pass well to the south, and much trade to be gained with the Kootenai Indians over the mountains if I can establish our company on the other side. But the Peigan will oppose that because those two tribes are hereditary enemies, and they fear us providing guns to their foes.

"Ilona's father is a man of some influence among the Peigan, although whether sufficient to counter Savard and his muskets we shall have to see. Still, we must try. The problem is that Savard is trying to put his claim on the girl, and with the old man unwell and in debt to the Bay, that is a complication better avoided.

"I propose to solve the debt problem by paying off old Baptiste's markers with the Bay, but we still must find time to forestall whatever Savard's plans are until more of our people arrive in mid-summer. If Three Bears is dead, as you say, and his eldest son as well, it will make it that much harder for Savard to foment trouble, but be assured he will manage it if he can, and we must do what we can to forestall him."

The factor, looking older than his thirty-five years, bent seriously over his pipe, his eyes flickering from Garth to the girl, Ilona, and back again.

"If we pay Baptiste's debts, and if we remove this young woman from Savard's . . . *attention,* I believe we can hold off any real problems with the Blackfoot until next year, if not beyond that. But it means Ilona must leave here and go to somewhere there is safety for her. Somewhere Savard has little or no influence, and the Bay none at all.

"Do you think the two of you could make it, alone, down to Boggy Hall? There is no nearby Hudson's Bay post, and I doubt if even Savard could intimidate old McIntyre, our company's factor there. You would have to travel overland, of course, since we couldn't spare a canoe even if we had one small enough. And you would have to leave now, while Savard is seeking out your former captors. I believe he might try to follow you, hopefully alone but most likely with those damnable Cardinal brothers. Still, if you leave well before Savard can be expected to return, and travel very quickly and cover your tracks with all the skills you have—"

The girl still had not looked squarely at Garth, who by this time was too intent on the words of his factor to notice, but she chose that moment to speak up, and her husky, lilting voice jarred him like a spur.

"It is not necessary for you to come. I can make such a trip alone," she said with a flash of eyes like wet coal. But for all her bravado, he could see that she was terrified, although whether of the journey or simply of the brute Savard, he couldn't tell.

"You will not go alone, and that is that," said the factor. "If your father were healthier . . . no, even then I would want someone along, and this young man is among my best. I would trust him with my own children, and I will trust him with your safety."

The look he flashed at Garth was silent but spoke volumes—a demand that this young woman's virtue would be protected, respected, and honored . . . or else!

Turning to meet the girl's anthracite eyes, any objections Garth might have had disappeared into the intensity of her gaze.

"I . . . uhm . . . I'll need clothes, first," he managed to mumble.

"I am working on them. They will be ready by morning." Whereupon she lowered her eyes and became the more typical, submissive Indian woman.

"Right. Settled, then." Thompson's voice revealed his

pleasure; his scowl continued a warning to Garth regarding future behavior. "Now, out of here, both of you," he said. "Cameron, you will need supplies, weapons, and you had best speak with the other men about the best and fastest route for your journey. And be careful who you talk to; I doubt any of our people would support Savard, but still . . . Be glad, at least, that we have sufficient decent horses; that Blackfoot nag you rode in on is barely half alive."

CHAPTER FIVE

Several days later, the sky painted with pink in the east, they quietly walked their horses out behind the post and pointed them north along the fishing trail to Crimson Lake.

The girl rode first on a small but wiry pinto selected by old René as the company's best, while Garth followed on a tall, rangy bay. At the end of a long rope snubbed to his saddle-bow was an enormous dun pack horse, described by Pierre as, "mean as the devil himself, but the son-of-a-bitch fears nothing on two legs or four, and if worst comes to worst he'll carry you both to Fort Augustus and be fresher than you when he arrives."

Ilona had donned Blackfoot-style leggings under her short doeskin tunic and rode astride with easy competence. Somewhere, she had acquired a poncho made from an old trade blanket, but even this failed to hide from her young escort the occasional titillating glimpse of smooth, flexing thighs. Garth was dressed like a chief, by comparison, in the fine new elk-skin shirt and leggings Ilona had crafted for him. Wrapped in his saddle roll were the other clothes René had arranged for, and on his head was a cap of coonskin traded from a southern Peigan.

The horses were gaunt from winter but moved along steadily. Threading through the windfall timber he knew would be all too common along the lake, Garth didn't expect to make ten miles a day, and their only safe route would be the long way round.

From Rocky Mountain House to the post below Blue Rapids on the Saskatchewan was a two-day journey by canoe, but for them it would take better than a week, since they had to swing in a large semi-circle to avoid the wintering grounds of the Sunchild Cree, who ranged an area from Brewster Creek to the Brazeau along the west bank of the river. Peaceable enough in their trading, they were fiercely possessive about their hunting grounds and known to have provided unpleasant deaths to white men who had dared to trap within their territory.

Avoiding them meant a journey of at least seventy-five miles extra, and Garth knew the chances of a spring blizzard or other incident could stretch that by half again. Ilona's father had once been through this country, but few others had tried such a journey away from the river, and Garth expected a rough trip.

Apart from a simple nod at his, "Ready?" that morning, Ilona had said nothing. Garth was too busy keeping the cantankerous pack beast in line to speak with her during the first day's trek but suggested they make another mile or two before stopping for the night, "just in case." This comment also brought nothing but a silent nod.

Camp made, supper half over, and the tea pail at the boil, Ilona still was silent and had barely so much as looked at Garth. Unsure if she was being coy or might be truly afraid of him, he was trying to decide how to deal with the situation when the sound of a fast-moving horse brought him to his feet in a rush, reaching for his rifle even as he kicked the fire apart to plunge the little clearing into relative darkness.

The ponies were looking up inquisitively, but without noise, and Ilona had disappeared into the adjoining spruce thicket when the oncoming rider pulled up, apparently uncertain of the trail. Garth could scarcely see the incoming animal against the night sky but was ready to chance a shot, anyway, when a familiar voice came to him from his left, unguarded side.

"You would not be for shooting at old René, would you?" The cackling whisper was followed by the small voyageur's familiar grating laugh.

"What the hell are you doing riding around in the middle of the night? Are you trying to get killed, you crazy old bastard?"

"*Le patron,* he send me to ride along with you. I think it is perhaps he fears for the virtue of your companion," the older man replied with a chuckle. "And I'm think he is probably right, too, but there is more. Savard, he is ride in at noon, and at once the trouble she starts. When he finds you are gone, little one,"—and he looked squarely at where Ilona thought herself safely concealed—"he is *tres* angry, and swears he will hunt you down and take you for himself. He makes no sense, that man . . . sometimes he sounds like he wants to bring ponies to your father's lodge, but then . . ." René shook his head in apparent confusion and turned his attention to Garth.

"*Le patron,* he says it might be best if you are warned that you no longer have the three-day start you had planned on, so he send me to warn you. And I think also he wants you to take a little guidance from an old woods-runner like me, eh?"

Ten minutes later, they were packed up and gone, leaving no trace of their brief camp. René had brought along his own gear, meager for the long journey but sufficient for his needs. They let the girl lead the way while the two men tried to form a strategy for dealing with those now certain to be on their trail.

At dawn, they were threading their way along the Baptiste River when René pulled his pony up sharply, motioning the others ahead. He rejoined them later, wearing a cherubic but wicked smile and carrying a bundle of arrow-length alder shoots.

"We make a few little traps, eh? Maybe they don't work, but if we are lucky, maybe Savard he doesn't watch close and he gets an arrow in his fat belly. A thong across the trail for a trigger and a bent branch for a bow . . . simple. And if nothing else, maybe it slows him down for a bit, although such a big belly I should not be able to miss."

They left half a dozen such traps along their trail, not really expecting even the first to accomplish much except to create caution and therefore slow down the pursuit.

Warm winds during the second and third days of their journey dried the hillsides and helped to erase the carefully planned trail René's expert woodsman's eye plotted. Working steadily to the north, they tried to avoid any contact with the Sunchild Cree, yet skirt their territory so closely that Savard would have to risk an encounter if he attempted any shortcuts aimed at catching them quickly.

Ilona still seemed to be avoiding Garth, although she often laughed shyly at some joke shared with René in the French tongue Garth had never really managed to master. Too often, indeed, he became convinced their jests were aimed at him but couldn't follow the dialogue enough to be sure. He did learn, however, that the girl's Indian name translated to *Climbing Woman*, and that she had actually been east to school for a time, and when she chose to, she could speak as good English as himself and infinitely better French, Cree, and Peigan Blackfoot.

Their stopovers on the trek were brief, averaging four hours before dawn and a short nap with the noon meal. They knew Savard had to be following, but since even he couldn't track at night, they made the most of every hour's travel the ponies could tolerate. Ilona, her native upbringing a credit under such travel conditions, took control of their brief camps. She hauled the water, did the cooking, and made the fires, leaving to Garth and René only the horse-handling as their portion of the work.

They lived on pemmican, bannock, and tea, not wanting to risk gunfire that could attract either Savard or the Cree. Early on the sixth day, René said he thought he saw smoke from the vicinity of their last camp, but a morning haze wiped out the vision so quickly that he wasn't sure it mightn't have been his imagination. Even so, they were extra cautious about their tracks that day and the next.

They met the Cree at the main ford on the Nordegg, and from almost the first moment, things went from bad to worse with a rush.

It was only a small party, led by the crippled Small Bear, still the band's war leader despite a badly twisted leg, the result of a careless encounter many years earlier with a sow grizzly and her cubs. Small Bear was an infrequent visitor to Rocky Mountain House, but he knew René and, without hesitation, rode down to the riverside to speak with the small voyageur. The rest of his party, however, milled about on the high ground, fingering their weapons ominously and muttering amongst themselves.

Garth missed the bulk of the sign language between René and Small Bear but got enough to sense the urgency it created in Ilona's dark eyes. She apparently knew what was involved in the crippled chief's proposal; ever since the talk began she had been edging her pony slowly downstream, away from both her escorts and the Cree on the other side.

When Small Bear's arm-waving climaxed with an emphatic grunt, she pivoted the horse in mid-stream and headed back, riding low in the saddle and pounding the horse with her heels. Garth had his horse turned half around when René shouted, and a shot rang out. Stunned, he sat still for an instant as he saw Ilona slump from her plunging pony to land with a splash of blood in the river. He dived from his own horse and caught her limp body before it had floated more than ten feet, but even as he gasped at the mask of blood pouring from her temple, something crashed in his own head, and blackness followed.

★　★　★　★　★

Garth awoke in darkness, cloud covering the sky and only the soft glow of banked coals visible of his surroundings. Throwing off the blanket that covered him, he lurched upright but was flattened by nausea before he was halfway up.

Then René was there, bringing cool water. Garth tried to speak, tried to ask about Ilona, but the effort was too much, and he slipped again into blackness.

. . . and then he was riding, high on a tall, bay horse, and every step hammered nails into his skull. Ilona was there, always ahead of him and never looking back, never speaking. He called, but she wouldn't listen, and her back was covered in welts and the part in her braided, raven hair was red with blood, not vermilion. He called again, and this time she did turn, but now she had no face, only a sudden red blotch that seemed to sag from her hair to the top of her deerskin tunic, and he screamed . . .

"Softly, softly . . ."

A cool cloth passed over his brow, and he looked up to find René looming over him, an anxious expression on his face.

"Ilona?" Garth asked but already knew what the answer must be. Regardless of his nightmare, he had seen the blood as she fell.

"I think maybe she is dead. I do not know. She floated downriver after you were shot, and the Cree, they would not let me look for her. They did not look, either, but even if she was not killed outright, she must be dead by now. It was three days ago."

"Three days! Where the hell are we?"

"Last night, we crossed the Brazeau, and the Cree they started back. We should reach the forks and maybe Boggy Hall within two days. If you can ride."

★　★　★　★　★

It took them four days, with Garth strapped onto the hastily improvised *travois* that René had created after the shooting. The bullet had creased above his left ear, slightly fracturing the skull but not too serious except for impairing his sense of balance to the point where he could hardly sit a horse without falling off one side or the other.

Small Bear's Cree had taken them straight north, meaning they had to cross the Brazeau at its most northern swing en route to the North Saskatchewan, and their return to the main river took them almost due south at one point. No matter how much they discussed the matter, they couldn't determine exactly what had happened during the shooting. René was sure the shots had come from their own side of the river, and Garth remembered little except that what he had heard sounded more like a proper rifle than a musket.

"I can only think it must have been Savard," he eventually declared. "If it had been the Cree, they would have gone after Ilona, and somebody from another band—the Cree would have been after *them,* not running us out of their territory."

"Savard, he was involved somehow, it is for certain," René agreed. "That Small Bear, he tried to lay claim on the girl, but he would not do that for himself. I'm thinking Savard put him up to it, but they did not want us to know about that."

"But if it was Savard, why shoot her? Surely he wouldn't want her dead! Unless he was aiming for her horse. He sure as hell wasn't aiming for mine, I can tell you that. That last shot was meant to kill."

"And almost did. But I am like you. I can think of no reason he would want to shoot the girl. It must have been a poor shot aimed at the horse. Or maybe even at you. There is no doubt that Savard wants this little Climbing Woman, but I am not sure if he wants to court her or buy her or steal her. And worse—I wonder if *he* knows, either."

"Well if he *has* killed her, I'll find the bastard and cut his heart out, I swear it," Garth snarled. And wordlessly revealed to his more experienced companion that this mixed-blood woman had influenced him more than even Garth, himself, realized.

Garth's raving swiftly drained his small store of energy, and within minutes he was sleeping heavily and without dreams. René, however, sat long by the dying fire, reflecting upon the impulsiveness of youth and recalling the many Indian "wives" he'd had during his years on the rivers.

Most voyageurs took up with Indian women at one time or another, there being no real choice if they wanted or needed feminine company. Often the practice was encouraged by the companies, since a man with a bed partner was less likely to cause trouble at the posts, or desert. Some, when it was time to return to the east, had taken their women and children along, but generally the temporary wives were left to rejoin their tribes or take up with some other man. Some Indian women had several children by as many different fathers. Nobody worried about that aspect of life in the wilderness, and the children were valued by all.

Even David Thompson, *le patron,* had a wife of mixed blood. His wife Charlotte was a daughter of a North West Company *bourgeoisie* from Lac la Biche and already had given him three children.

Women, René mused, were a convenience, but not indispensable. And yet . . . there had been that Plains Cree woman, many years ago along the South Saskatchewan. He had actually married that one, even though the marriage was *à la façon du pays*—in the fashion of the country—an Indian marriage by Indian customs and without the benefit of clergy, since there were no clergy for thousands of miles. He had called her Collette; now he couldn't remember her proper name. But if the measles hadn't taken her . . .

"Ah, this business of love is for the young ones, not an old man like me," he muttered and, rolling in his blankets, was asleep in seconds.

They arrived at Boggy Hall the next afternoon, Garth weaving in the saddle but insistent he would not arrive riding in a *travois* like an invalid or an old man. This was David McIntyre's post, and the dour old Scot's passion for neatness and order showed throughout the establishment. There was no welter of garbage and litter around the dock, and the many log buildings were freshly mudded and chinked with care.

McIntyre met them at the gate, scowling at the rude bandage around Garth's temples, but offering no welcome.

"So, 'tis wounded the lad is. Well, I'll give ye water and bandages and a meal, then ye must be on your way. 'Tis no room I have for cowards and scoundrels at my post, even if ye do be company men."

René's soft-spoken request for an explanation of the old man's attitude was drowned by Garth's shout of outrage.

"Cowards and scoundrels? What the hell are you talking about, old man? If you're not careful who you call names, I'll come down off this horse and teach you better manners," he shouted, ignoring his companion's call for calm.

" 'Tis what I said and what I meant, so guard your tongue, lad. We've all heard here how you abandoned Baptiste's girl to the Cree and ran for your craven lives. I've spoken to the girl, and she does nae deny it. If not for Savard—and I'm no champion of that one, believe me, but the evidence on this is clear—the girl could be dead this day, instead of on her way home to her father at Rocky Mountain House. Now get your head looked after, feed yourselves, and then get off my post."

With which old McIntyre turned on his heel and stalked

back to his personal cabin, paying no attention to Garth's protests. His men were no more pleasant, despite some of them knowing René from years past. The cook slopped a meal before them with a muttered curse, and the post medical man used a minimum of gentleness in re-bandaging Garth's head. Nobody would speak to them or answer their questions about Ilona's condition or how she and Savard had come to Boggy Hall.

René's request for fresh horses to hasten their journey upriver drew nothing from McIntyre but a further demand that they leave his post immediately if not sooner. Weak as he was, Garth would have seized upon it as an excuse for a fight, but the old Frenchman's cooler head prevailed. Within the hour they were riding their tired ponies down to the ford and looking for the eastern trail that might lead them back to Rocky Mountain House without further meeting the Cree.

They splashed across the ford at Rocky Mountain House a week later, arriving to an unexpected hostility even from their own people, the shouts of derision from the Bay men being hardly surprising. Only the presence of David Thompson, known and respected by all, kept their arrival from being the catalyst for an all-out war between the companies, and one in which some of his own men might have had difficulty choosing sides.

"You had best explain yourselves and do it quickly," was Thompson's critical opening remark when Garth and René had been ushered through a barrage of angry looks into the relative security of *le patron*'s own cabin. Two hours later, after much accusation and counter-accusation, the factor had accepted their story but had no solution for the impending clash shaping up outside.

"There is no way around it. You'll have to leave this post at once," Thompson advised. "Savard, saints be praised, is away somewhere himself, and with all of you away from here, the men will let the incident blow over, at least for now. The girl is safe with her father, not too badly hurt but obviously too frightened to speak of what happened. Or maybe she doesn't remember, as she insists. But until she is able to confirm your story and explain Savard's involvement, the Bay men will try to use the incident as an excuse for causing trouble.

"It is also possible," he said, glowering down at his extinguished pipe and shaking his head with worry, "that even the girl believes Savard's story. If what you've said is correct, she probably has no more idea than you do who shot her or why."

"It had to have been Savard," Garth insisted. "The Cree didn't have rifles, only muskets, and *we* sure as hell didn't shoot at her."

Thompson ignored him, turning his attention instead to René.

"Giroux, I hold you partially responsible," he said. "You should have fled at the first sign Small Bear wanted to trade for the girl. But then, I suppose you couldn't know she would understand the sign talk that well."

"What I do not understand, me, is why Small Bear wanted the girl," René countered. "It can only be that somehow Savard, he was involve in that, too."

"Too late now to worry about that. The damage is done," replied the factor. "Now, it is growing dusk. I want you two to remain inside this cabin. I will have food sent to you and fresh horses prepared, but I will not chance you wandering around the camp and furthering this uproar. I think I will have to send you north on a mission to scout out new trading possibilities. But for now, you stay here."

He strode impatiently from the cabin, but the door had hardly swung shut than it was thrown open again to admit Ilona's father, old Jean-Paul Baptiste, looking twice as old as when they had last seen him only weeks before.

"*Nisih kach*—gently, gently. I bring you no harm," he said. "If there is harm to be done, let us save it for that *apeht awi kosisan;* that son-of-a-bitch Savard. I know you didn't abandon my girl, and I am equally sure you did not shoot her. Especially not this young man here, eh?" he said with a wry grin at Garth. "You had other plans, hey, large one? The same as Savard, perhaps, but with a good deal more gentleness, I'd wager."

Then he became deadly serious, gesturing toward the outside with a bleak look. "I think I can calm the men down. In both camps, they know me, and they know Jean-Paul Baptiste does not lie. But you had best be gone, anyway, before that Savard returns, because *le patron* he is right that the Bay men will use this as an excuse for a fight."

He was interrupted by the sound of shooting from the Hudson's Bay Post, then nearly trampled as both Garth and René charged toward the door. They were halted, however, by the return of David Thompson, who scowled at their obvious intentions but said nothing as he motioned them back inside. All four men then sat in fidgety silence until André Charbonneau, one of the chief traders, burst in.

"*Mon Dieu!* It has finally happen," he said. "That pig Savard has killed one of his own company's men and then has wounded *le factor* of the Bay post. Bird has a bullet in him, and Savard, he has fled with those weasels, the Cardinal brothers. Bird's entire post is in an uproar; his men they are shoot at shadows out there. *Sacré!* It is not safe to be in the woods there tonight.

"And," he added almost as an afterthought, having obviously just noticed Baptiste's presence in the cabin. "He has taken your girl—"

Garth and the old man were already halfway to the door when they were halted by a curt command from David Thompson.

"Cameron! Sit down! And you, too, Baptiste. Nothing is to

49

be gained by storming out of here on a blind trail at night. Especially not with the Bay people ready to shoot at any sound they hear. You will rest out the night, and in the morning we will talk more of this.

"Charbonneau . . . bring food. And a tot of rum for our young man here. I think he could stand it. Matter of fact, I think we all could.

"Show some sense, young Cameron. The trail will not be cold by morning, and you need rest more than a wild goose chase now. By the morning you could make twenty miles in the wrong direction or get yourself shot before you pass the Bay post. So eat, rest, and then be off with the sun . . . in the right direction."

Garth wanted to argue, wanted to leave *now* and to hell with the dangers, but his common sense came to the fore, and he reluctantly agreed. Several tots of rum later, he was still half-inclined to rush off into the night, but now his body wouldn't obey his brain, and soon he was curled up asleep.

CHAPTER SIX

Ilona squirmed frantically in the harsh grasp of Elzear Cardinal. The foul-smelling little half-breed balanced her easily across his saddle-bow, and her writhing did little to upset the effortless balance he kept on the swift little mountain pony.

Nor did her movements hinder his grasping, groping hands as he clutched almost rhythmically at her breasts and crotch and whispered obscenities in her ear whenever it seemed Savard wouldn't notice.

The massive Savard, in the confusion of the escape from Acton House, had been unable to take his usual mount, a seventeen-hand stallion with a build and temperament well matched to that of his huge master. The runty roan Savard had caught up in his rush to depart couldn't possibly carry both the two-hundred-eighty-pound woodsman and the girl, so he'd delegated the younger Cardinal brother to carry Ilona.

Twisting away from a harsh pinch by Cardinal, Ilona found her mouth only inches from his ear, and, without really thinking of the possible consequences, she grasped the lobe between her strong young teeth and ripped savagely away with the next lurch of the pony.

"*Oskanuk* . . . bitch!" he screamed, throwing Ilona to the ground and leaping from the startled pony to beat and kick at her. Blood streaming from his torn ear, he pulled Ilona up by one of her braids and was methodically kicking her when Savard struck him down with a rifle butt.

His face a mask of fury, the huge woods boss leaped from his horse and smashed Elzear again and again across the face with his fist, cursing at him in a mixture of Cree and gutter French. When the younger Cardinal dropped unconscious, Savard left him sprawled in the trail. He then dragged up the youth's pony and slung Cardinal across the saddle like a bag of grain.

Grasping Ilona about the waist, he threw her up to the other Cardinal brother. Savard snarled, "If you lay one hand on her, you shit-eating half-breed pup, I will break your head like your brother's. This woman is mine . . . do you understand that? Mine! Now, let us be away from here, and if that young squirt of a brother of yours cannot keep up, he can damned well stay behind. I have no time for cripples."

It was an attitude that did little to ease Ilona's fears, although she was far from being crippled. Her head wound had been nasty looking but superficial and was nearly healed. The bullet had ticked her forehead at the hairline, and, while there had been much blood at the time and she had been stunned and disoriented, she had been almost recovered by the time Savard returned her to Rocky Mountain House. Her problem now was in trying to fathom why he had bothered to do so, if only to steal her himself before hardly a week had passed. It made no sense, but the danger of her present circumstances was only too clear!

She noted that Elzear, beginning to regain his wits by this time, had found some common sense with them. Although he threw barbed looks at Savard through eyes swollen nearly shut from the beating, he stayed sprawled across the saddle and kept his mouth shut.

They rode through the night and most of the next day, following game trails as much as possible, but staying far enough from the river to avoid any chance meetings with roving Indians. Savard planned to skirt the Blackfoot country, then pull north along the mountains toward the Athabasca, where he knew there would be a chance of meeting other Hudson's Bay Company parties sooner or later.

Young Elzear rode virtually blind for the next six days, his eyes swollen shut from Savard's beating. Little time was taken to care for him, although his brother Lucien bathed his eyes whenever they stopped to water the horses. Lucien, unlike his brother, left Ilona unmolested. He knew Savard's ugly temper and knew death would follow further provocation of the big man.

A decent camp was demanded by the eighth day, as their meager food supply was exhausted and the ponies virtually useless from stumbling along pitted moose trails without sufficient rest or food.

Ilona was at a loss to understand Savard's purpose in kidnapping her. Whilst returning her from Boggy Hall to Rocky Mountain House, he had treated her with a curiously gentle courtesy, helping her up and down from her horse—the same horse she'd been riding when she'd been shot, although she had no idea how the beast had come into Savard's possession. He'd done the camp chores himself, cooked their meals, and—strangest of all—had spoken barely a word to her during the entire journey.

He'd seemed . . . shy, more than anything. As if he had no experience with women, didn't know what to say or how to say it. He was, however, always aware of her, seldom taking his eyes from her when not being alert to the trail and their surroundings. She'd been constantly aware of his scrutiny, of being watched, studied, analyzed.

But never touched. Not once did he put his hands on her in any way that threatened, or seemed inappropriate, or even worrying . . . except . . .

When she'd first returned to consciousness after being shot, she'd opened her eyes to see what might have been the eyes of a gigantic black bear, staring down at her from only inches away. Eyes of a unique auburn coloring, but eyes of such gentle expression she had felt no fear, no concerns. Initially.

In her ears was the echo of a whisper, a plea, perhaps a name. "Francine," she thought it was, repeated over and over in an echo of sorrow, of loss, but also something else. Something gentle as the fingers that stroked her hair away from the wound, huge fingers that should have been clumsy but were deft and knowing as they cleansed the gash at her hairline and daubed her incision with a pungent mixture of herbs and pine sap.

There was a gentle adoration in his gaze, but that was so at odds with everything she knew of the hulking woodsman; Ilona had no idea how to interpret it. It made her feel almost infantile, in some ways, but her innate sensuality was in there somewhere, and his awareness of that made her cautious, kept her on edge throughout their return to Rocky Mountain House.

She'd made that journey with at least a semblance of normalcy, but now . . . now was not the same. Now was . . . terrifying, if only because now was en route to a destination all too easy to imagine. And to fear.

Their speedy progress had denied any chance to hunt, so Savard ordered the Cardinals to guard the girl and set up camp while he searched for game. Elzear's face, by this time, had healed enough that he could see and talk without too much pain. They bedded the horses in a nearby meadow, tied Ilona to a tree, and slunk to the far edge of camp for a conference.

"That bastard! I will kill him yet for this . . . and then I will have the girl," snarled Elzear.

"Ugh! Enough talk of killing. Even for both of us it would be a matter of much risk. Besides, you should have known better than to fool with the girl, anyway," replied Lucien. "Savard has the only good rifle among us, and he knows where he is going. This country is new to me, and I do not like it. We will let him lead us to wherever he is going and *then* maybe kill him. But, for now, let well enough alone. There are plenty of girls, and this one isn't worth getting yourself killed over."

"*Oui,* but why should we follow him *north*? There is nothing there for us but a bunch of Woods Cree that are likely as not to want our scalps . . . or worse."

Elzear paused, rubbing gingerly at his swollen earlobe. "And I want *that* woman. There is no reason Savard should have her first. I want her—and I will have her!"

A crashing of brush announced the return of Savard, who stomped into the camp with a hind quarter of moose slung over one shoulder. He carried the two-hundred-pound ham like a twig, twirling it expertly from his shoulder with one hand and muttering commands at his followers even before the meat hit the ground.

"Untie the girl and set her to cooking this meat," he said. "It was a fat, dry cow and well worth the bullet. Lucien, go out there and get the other hind quarter and the tenderloin. We might need the extra meat before we have another chance to stop like this. There is a creek a half mile to the west, and the moose is maybe three bends upstream.

"Elzear, stop sulking like a wounded pup and get that fire stirred up. By the gods, we will eat well tonight. I think there is even some salt left."

The meal was simple—moose meat and more of the same. Ilona had to force herself to eat despite her fears, but the three men ate like they'd been starved for days.

Savard slashed steaks from the fresh carcass in three-inch strips, eating the first one nearly raw while the rest broiled on green sticks over the fire. He ate as he did everything else, with a vigorous dexterity that belied his immense bulk.

The Cardinals ate, belched, then returned to their meat in typical savage gluttony. Lucien swallowed more than three pounds of half-raw moose meat before throwing it up again. Undaunted, he speared another chunk from the fire and put it to his grease-stained face with a weak gesture at his brother to do the same.

Lucien had also brought in the nose of the animal, singed it briefly in the flames, and it simmered in a hastily-contrived pot of birch bark caulked with pitch.

The flames faded slowly, hissing to renewed life with each spurt of dripping fat from the chunks of meat spitted on the green sticks. At one corner of the camp, Lucien Cardinal snored and belched his way through a restless slumber. By the fire, Savard snored easily, unaffected by the smoldering glances aimed his way from the hooded eyes of Elzear Cardinal.

Ilona, once again tied to the tree, tried to sleep, but she was all too aware of Elzear Cardinal's scrutiny and feared it. She closed her eyes for only a brief moment, it seemed, then was startled awake to an awareness of pure terror as her mouth was blocked by a greasy hand and her ears assaulted by crude suggestions she could only half understand.

Although she realized it was hopeless, she kicked and squirmed and tried to bite at the hard, foul-tasting hand. The only sound she could utter was a strangled grunt—enough noise to rouse Savard. The big man leapt to his feet with the grace of a hunting cougar, his knife ready in one huge fist and curses rumbling from his throat.

"Elzear, you bastard! Damn it, why don't you learn? This time, by God, I'll kill you. Stinking little half-breed whelp. I told you the girl is mine. But you don't listen. You never listen. So now I think I'll cut off your pathetic little balls and stuff them down your throat."

His dusky face blanched by fear, Elzear abandoned Ilona and swept his own knife in low arcs as he circled the dying fire. It was obvious he feared any fight with the giant Savard, but equally obvious all choice was gone. He said nothing Ilona could understand, only mumbled grunts deep in his throat.

Savard moved without haste, kicking the edges of the fire to produce better light. The keen blades flashed in the glow as the two figures slowly circled, not yet engaged but making small, flickering jabs with their knives.

Surprisingly to Ilona, Elzear made no attempt to involve his brother in the dispute, but she noticed that Savard moved always so as to keep them both in his sight, with the fire between himself and Elzear, with Lucien on his flank, but where Savard could see him . . . and well out of reach.

All was quiet but for Elzear and Savard's breathing, the whisper of their moccasins in the grass, and the crackle of the half-roused coals. Lucien made no attempt to aid his brother, and once, when Savard glanced his way, he shrugged his lack of involvement with spread hands and a downcast gaze. Savard's contemptuous sneer told Ilona he trusted neither the suggestion of neutrality nor the cowardly brother of his opponent.

And then, with a terrifying suddenness, it was over. Savard kicked ashes toward the younger Cardinal brother, then in a single pounce was across the fire in a slashing attack upon the smaller man. A single, choking shriek, and Elzear Cardinal was on his knees before the flames, clutching at a spreading pile of his own entrails with both hands and making little mewing sounds of agony. One kick from Savard's large, moccasined foot toppled him on his side as the firelight dimmed and Elzear's eyes grew vacant.

"Now, damn it, do you want some of that, too?" Savard roared at Lucien, who'd not moved from his blankets. "If the answer is no, throw this fool's body out for the wolves and start packing up this camp. It is time to move."

Hatred burned in the eyes of Lucien Cardinal—Ilona could see it, almost taste it even if Savard seemed not to notice. But Lucien said nothing as he dragged his brother's corpse to a nearby gully, then stalked away and began to un-hobble the ponies.

CHAPTER SEVEN

The raucous braying of a flock of ravens drew Garth and René to Savard's campsite two days later. They sat their horses at the edge of the camp and stared silently for long moments at the coyote-strewn remains of Elzear Cardinal.

"This is one less we have to fight, I am thinking," René said with a shrug. "From the signs, it was only this one against Savard, but in truth he must have had little chance. Savard, he is one bad brute."

More ravens guided them to the moose carcass, now bloated beyond recovery in the hot mountain sun and already stinking so badly it could be smelled for half a mile.

"This I do not like," muttered René. "We are having to live on pemmican, and not much of that. These others, they have good moose meat to keep them strong. It is not good. That Savard, he is already too strong."

"Yes, and look at all the wolf tracks. There will be precious little game in the country ahead if that is any indication," said Garth.

Seeking to put distance between themselves and the stinking, bear-bait carcasses, they pushed their horses hard throughout that day and at dusk were well into the side hills of the Nikanassin Mountains. Seeking a place to make an inconspicuous camp, René walked his pony to the edge of a nearby ridge. Looking down, he noted immediately a broad trail that had seen a lot of recent heavy use.

"*Mon Dieu!* Come and look at this," he hissed to Garth. "It was no moose that made this road. Either we are onto the Cree highway, or else . . . that is it . . . this is the main trail north to the medicine springs. Myself, I have never been there, but many times I hear of this place from the northern Cree. And even from some Blackfoot. At the north end of these mountains, I think . . . high up. There is water boiling right out of the rock, and stinks like the pits of hell, or so they say, but for the old ones, especially, there is good medicine there. And look! This track here, with the broken frog in the off hind foot . . . that is the runty little mare Elzear Cardinal was riding. For sure I don't forget that track. They are ahead of us, but now I'm thinking we can make better time because we know where Savard is headed. The medicine springs. And I'm betting they will lay over a day or so there, because that small horse he is riding must be about dead from the load."

Three days later, chilly in the pre-dawn cold, Garth and René walked their ponies up to the last crest before the gorge where hot springs spewed up sulfurous steam into an almost sterile landscape. A clear view was impossible, so they squatted near the crest until the rising sun had burned off the night vapors.

"I am not liking the way Savard seemed to turn off the trail back there maybe a day ago," René mused. "Either he was planning to scout this place before coming in, which maybe puts us ahead of him, or he doesn't even know of it, and he's going round the mountain."

"I think maybe we passed him," said Garth. "They weren't moving all that fast, from the tracks. I'll bet they show up later today . . . or even maybe tomorrow. Anyway, our own horses need rest, too. Let's find a decent place where they can graze, and then we'll come back and keep an eye on this trail. That shower last night will have wiped out our tracks, so we should be able to stay out of sight. You wait and see . . . they'll show up later today or early tomorrow. God, what I'd give for some of that moose meat right now. I wonder if they've got any left."

CHAPTER EIGHT

Lucien Cardinal would have shot both Garth and René as they passed on the medicine trail, a scant thirty-five yards from where Lucien, Ilona, and Savard lay hidden behind a willow thicket. But Savard said no, and his word brooked no argument.

"*Non,*" he whispered in a voice that seemed much too soft to have emerged from his massive throat. "It is too easy that way." He emphasized his viewpoint with the point of his knife against the small half-breed's throat.

"I will kill that young one myself . . . with these two hands." The sadistic glee in his eyes made even Lucien Cardinal, who knew the big man's penchant for violence, shudder inside.

"They will stop at the medicine springs, and we can ambush them there," Savard continued, once Garth and René had passed them by and would be out of hearing. "There, you can kill the old monkey any way you want, but the young one is mine!"

Lucien knew better than to argue, but the big man's logic was wasted on him. Lucien was typical of his society, brave enough when bravery was the only option, but conditioned to the Indian belief that it was no sign of bravery to take unnecessary risks. Among his people, respect belonged to the warrior who outsmarted his enemy, and there was no shame in shooting him in the back, unseen and without risk. Such action was a sign of good judgment and wisdom.

Lucien knew Savard's tremendous strength and his love of

violent hand-to-hand combat, but even the dozen or more times he'd watched the big man crush others in his hands didn't lessen his view that it was a foolish way to fight.

Never had he seriously questioned Savard's leadership. Ever since their first meeting years before, on the lower Saskatchewan, both Lucien and his brother had followed the brutal Savard with blind faithfulness . . . jackals behind a lion. They had guarded his back, stolen for him, even killed for him. And lived on the leavings he threw them, including any number of women over the years. But . . .

"This . . . this is too much," he muttered to himself as they settled into a dry camp that night. "First, he keeps the woman to himself and does not even use her. Then he kills Elzear for wanting her. Truly, the big one has gone mad."

Lucien's imagination strengthened that conviction throughout the evening as he lay awake long past full dark, searching his brain for a way to escape from the situation, preferably with the girl, but most importantly without suffering Savard's wrath in the process.

He knew the big man's hog-like snoring was deceptive. Savard's instincts were truly those of an animal, his sleep light, instinctively alert, all his senses tuned to potential danger. Moving about the camp, Lucien often had noticed Savard's suspicious, glittering eyes upon him when he would have sworn an instant earlier that the man was deep asleep. And, in his mind, he could still see the catlike bound with which Savard had cleared the fire to spill Elzear's guts with a single slashing gesture.

If Savard felt the uneasiness in camp, he gave no sign, but Ilona knew something was amiss. Everything in her Indian ancestry spoke to her of it. Death stalked this camp and teased at the horizons of her mind, and she shivered inwardly each time either of her captors stirred.

At seventeen, Ilona was already old to still be a maiden amongst her mother's people. Most girls of the Plains tribes reached puberty early and were mothers by the time they'd seen sixteen summers. Her father's influence and her own fierce pride had combined to save her that much, at least.

She had been born far to the east of the mountains and the post at Rocky Mountain House, deep in the rolling buffalo country near the forks of the Saskatchewan. Her grandmother had been a princess amongst the Peigan but had abandoned her heritage for the love of a French-Canadian voyageur, one of the first ever to strike west toward the towering mountains and the promise of a fortune in furs.

Ilona's mother, called Grouse Wing, had been a maiden of fourteen when the young Jean-Paul Baptiste came up the river with a bawdy glint in his eye and woman hunger burning in his loins. He spent the winter with Grouse Wing's people, and when the flood ice thundered loose in the spring, he resumed his westward voyage with the noticeably pregnant Peigan girl tucked amongst his traps in the bow of the canoe.

Jean-Paul was something of a rarity among the river-men. He'd spent his lusts in a hundred Indian lodges along the rivers between Montreal and the Rockies, but his strong Catholic upbringing demanded a more permanent relationship than the normal casual trysts of the voyageurs. After four years, each of them having given him one more strong, healthy son, he returned down river one spring in search of a black-robed priest to bless his union with Grouse Wing and to baptize his growing family.

There had been eleven children, eventually, of which only seven sons survived the harsh prairie winters and the other dangers of their lifestyle. Then Ilona arrived with the spring grass, and everything magically changed for the voyageur. All the boys had drawn richly from their Indian heritage, but the thriving girl-child took only the flashing dark eyes and raven hair. Her skin was as creamy as that of some redheads, and her hair, while it was the color of wet coal, was fine as fox fur. She'd been beautiful right from birth, and now at seventeen she would have been a stunning woman in any society.

Jean-Paul Baptiste received his first-born—and only—daughter as a blessing from heaven. He named her Ilona—her mother's people called her Climbing Woman—and gave her all his affections. He also did his best to ensure that she had something of an education, and he, himself, instructed her in his native Quebec French, along with such English as he had picked up over the years, and every possible aspect of every native language and dialect their wanderings encountered.

Approaching womanhood, she'd received her share of suitors but had turned down all of them—warrior, trapper, trader, or voyageur—with equal disdain. Her father was the best of the free trappers and had instructed her well in the role of frontier princess.

"One day," he told her, "a man will come to you. Not one of these slack-assed, ignorant river-men who are afraid of the forests and the Indians and everything that walks on land. This is a huge land and a cruel one, but not a land to be feared. It is heaven compared to the crowded villages of the east. You may see them one day, but you will not like them . . . people running everywhere like camp dogs seeking shelter from the rain.

"This is the country," he'd said, "where a brave man can spend his life with no worries and no *patron* to throw stupid orders at him, or try to run his life. The forest, it is filled with game, and the rivers are full of fish. What else could a strong man want, except maybe a little salt for his meat and enough beaver to keep him in traps and powder and ball?"

When they had come to the post at Acton House, he had

warned his lovely young daughter—harshly and in some detail—about the dangers a man like Savard could present for a young and pretty maiden.

"And those Cardinal brothers . . . *pftt!* Beasts, they are. Weasels who follow that pig Savard to lap up the blood he spills. They are considered vermin even amongst their own people. You must avoid all of them. It would be better to die than to be used by animals like that."

Ilona shuddered now at the current impact of her father's words. Glancing around the well-concealed campsite as she wrestled quietly with her bonds, she noticed Savard's ratty little roan gelding perk up its ears and shy from some unseen terror in the nearby scrub. The horse managed a single, muted whicker of fear that faded before a deadly roar as a huge grizzly reared out of the darkness and struck the pony down with a single, crushing blow.

Ilona screamed.

Lucien Cardinal scrambled erect with fear naked and trembling in his eyes, and Savard came out of his blankets with a cocked rifle in his hand, seeking a clear shot in the flickering moonlight.

The rifle barked, three foot of flame spouting from the muzzle, but the sound was lost, swallowed in the moaning roar of the giant bear. Then man and beast became a clawing, grunting tornado of fur and flesh, rolling through the tiny clearing and into the darkness outside the firelight.

Ilona was nearly paralyzed with fear, but as they rolled past her she saw Savard's knife flash and felt blood splashing on her. An instant later she was dragged erect by the hair and her tether cut by a different knife . . . this one in the hands of Lucien Cardinal. He muttered a command for quiet as he dragged her to the remaining horses, which shied in panic. Lucien threw her astride the pony his brother had ridden from Acton House and looped her tether around the horse's neck.

"You ride, bitch," he muttered savagely in her ear. "And do not stop until I do, or I'll cut your throat and throw you to the wolves. Now go!"

He slapped the terrified horse on the rump with his bared knife, threw hastily-gathered robes and camp goods on his own pony, and followed closely behind Ilona. All she could do was bend low on the horse's neck as it swung onto the medicine trail and turned north with bear stink in its nostrils and rank fear in its heart.

CHAPTER NINE

Savard emerged from beneath the stinking bear carcass bathed in blood but without any serious wounds. His single shot had broken the grizzly's spine and partially paralyzed the deadly forepaws, but even disabled, the animal in its final minutes had given Savard one of the toughest fights of his life.

His moose-hide shirt was torn to shreds, and his back was a mass of superficial scratches and scrapes. One shoulder had been bitten, and he had several lesser bites along his left arm.

"*Mon Dieu!* That was a fight to remember," he muttered as he clambered through the tangled underbrush to the campsite. "Cardinal! Tell that girl to heat water and get some spruce gum to help close these wounds . . ."

Elation faded to disbelief and then rage as he scanned the empty camp.

"*Sacré!* Dirty, half-breed son-of-a-bitch! I will kill you for this," he shouted. Charging about the camp in a frenzy, he determined that the horses were gone, but he still had his rifle, powder and ball, his knife and sundry other items abandoned during Cardinal's hasty departure with Ilona.

Muttering curses, Savard went to the creek, where he cleansed and dressed his wounds as well as he could, then wrapped himself in a spare blanket, gathered his weapons, and took up the trail.

He moved swiftly despite the loss of blood and by dawn had nearly reached the gully where the medicine springs bubbled from the rock in a sulfurous mist. The horse trail left by Cardinal and Ilona had branched off to the east, and, while Savard instinctively wanted to follow it, to smash his former follower into a bloody pulp, common sense quickly took hold. He was certain Garth Cameron and old René would have gone to the medicine springs in a bid to ambush him, and if they were still there he might be able to steal one of their horses, perhaps even kill them and steal all of their horses. At worst, he would be able to bathe his wounds in the healing waters and recover his strength.

Savard had lived in the wilderness, at times with the Ojibwa and Cree of the eastern forests and the Blackfoot and northern Sioux on the Great Plains. He knew that a determined man in good condition could walk down any horse, especially in mountain country where a man had the huge advantage of agility.

He knew also that the inherent laziness and superstitious nature of the remaining Cardinal brother could only work to Savard's advantage. Lucien's unfamiliarity with this region would slow the fleeing half-breed, who had few skills when it came to mountain travel. More important to Savard, he believed Cardinal's superstitious fear of him would keep the cowardly half-breed from messing with Ilona until he had reached somewhere he felt safe, where he could take his pleasure of her without having to watch his back in anticipation of Savard's fury.

"And if he is not careful, him, the little Climbing Woman will protect herself without me—she is a strong woman, that one," he muttered half aloud.

A narrow mountain-sheep trail gave sheltered access to the valley of the hot springs and allowed Savard to slink undetected upon the resting camp of Garth and René. Expert in the craft of ambush, he quickly scouted a route whereby he could shoot

René and grab all the horses without significant risks to himself. It seemed obvious the searchers would remain through that day, so Savard moved upstream of them to a place where he could rest and bathe his wounds in a small, half-hidden pool.

The luxury of the medicinal bath soaked away his aches, and he drifted into slumber even as he plotted his next moves.

Garth was becoming restless at the inactivity. He realized the horses needed the rest but chafed to be off again after Ilona. René's pony had picked up a stone bruise en route to the hot-springs canyon, and the elderly voyageur had decreed it would be senseless for them to continue without giving the animal time to recover.

"Do not be always in such a hurry," he cautioned his young friend. "Even if Savard don't come to this spring, we still can catch up again, but only if we have horses that are sound. The grass here is good, and we are well set up for an ambush if they do come. Give my horse one more day, and then we'll go on if you like, but it's you that will walk if the horse comes up lame again. Old René has walked enough in his lifetime."

They were sprawled in the sun beneath the rimrock, with the ponies grazing quietly in a hidden meadow two hundred yards below them. The main trail into the canyon lay a quarter mile below the horses, and they were concealed from it by a fringe of scrub juniper along the meadow. Garth's restlessness was amplified by the fact he'd not eaten a decent meal since their arrival at the springs. Several fat mountain sheep had roamed down from the crest, one of them close enough that Garth could have slain it with a bow and arrow—if he'd had one. But the possibility of ambushing Savard, slim as it was beginning to appear, precluded any risk of spoiling everything with the sound of a careless rifle shot, so both men had to make do with pemmican and water.

René, true to his nature, accepted the problem with a good dose of philosophy. If one could not travel because of a lame horse, he'd said, why worry about it at all? Life to him was filled with minor tribulations, and he'd found during his many years in the wilderness that fretting did nothing to help any situation. Accordingly, while Garth paced back and forth along the narrow rock ledge, René sprawled lazily in the warming sunshine, taking his rest while he could.

"This is a good place for old bones," he said. "The sun and the hot mineral water soothes many aches. I almost feel young again, but not so young and restless as you, young Cameron. *Sacré bleu!* Sit down. You make an old man nervous. What are you trying to do, make a target for Savard, or any trigger-happy Indian that wanders by? This is not the only trail to the basin, you know? I have been watching the sheep, and they come in by at least three different routes. I am thinking this is the best place for us to be, but if we become careless we would be fine targets up here. *N'est-ce pas?*"

He yawned prodigiously and was halfway sitting up when the bullet splattered rock splinters in his face.

Garth, crouching swiftly behind a rock, was seeking the source of that bullet when he became aware of muted moans from the old man. René was curled tightly on the ground, twisting and writhing with both hands to his face and blood coursing through his tightly-clenched fingers.

"*Nom de Dieu* . . . I cannot see," he whimpered. "Watch closely the horses. I'm thinking it is only rock dust in my eyes, but I cannot help you . . ." The words were drowned out by a drumming of hooves, and Garth looked down-slope to see both horses bounding through the far entrance to the meadow with Savard astride the smaller mount.

Garth managed a single, clumsy shot, which went wide, and before he could reload the horses were springing through an aspen thicket and into the thicker timber. Cursing, he threw down the rifle and turned to René. The little voyageur had ceased writhing but still had both hands clenched over his face and was making small, mewling sounds.

It was only after considerable argument that René allowed Garth to move his hands, and the younger man shuddered at the damage caused by Savard's rock-splattered bullet. René's entire face was a chopped mess of lead slivers, rock fragments, dirt, and blood.

Gathering their gear, Garth guided René down the ridge to the warmest of the springs gushing from the rock and tried to bathe away the mess. René, eyes clenched tightly throughout the process, made no sound, not even when Garth dug out a half-inch sliver of rock from his forehead. Once the old man's face was clean, it seemed to Garth that one splinter was the major source of the blood.

To the old man, however, it was a different story. Convinced his eyes had been struck, and fearing blindness, he steadfastly refused to open them despite Garth's pleas. He didn't argue, simply crouched like a gnome beside the steaming waters, his eyes squeezed shut and his body wracked by shudders.

Nothing Garth said or did seemed to be of any use, so he turned away and began sorting out their gear as he contemplated the long walk ahead of them. He cleaned and reloaded his rifle, stowed camp goods under a robe, and dragged René back away from the water. Issuing a muttered, "Stay here and don't move," he slipped away to investigate Savard's ambush.

He'd barely stepped through the fringe of aspen when a low whicker brought him up short. Peering through the tangled branches, he saw his own mare step into the meadow from the far side. Garth froze in his tracks, unable to see clearly beyond the mare and fearful of another ambush. Forcing himself to be patient, he waited a full ten minutes, watching as the mare grazed quietly toward him, then called her with an almost silent whistle that brought the horse prancing toward him.

He had no idea why Savard hadn't hung on to the bay mare, which should have been the big man's logical choice of a horse to steal and ride, but it seemed obvious she'd merely fled in the panic with René's much smaller mount, then decided not to bother staying with it.

They returned to the spring to find old René studiously bathing his eyes and crooning to himself in French patois. He looked up at Garth's approach, tears streaming down his cheeks from the strong sulfur water but obviously able to see again.

"Aha! That is a stroke of luck, *non*? That fat bastard Savard will get nowhere in a hurry on that stone-bruised cabbagehead I was riding. Even your mare couldn't stand his company, eh? Damn, that flying rock made a mess of my face. The small fuss I made, like a babe, for that I am sorry. You must forgive an old man his small fears."

He squinted at Garth as if to assure himself, then went on. "Old René has traveled from Montreal to these mountains three times, and he's not afraid of anything . . . not man, not beast, not the Blackfoot or the white-water rapids . . . but the blindness—yes! René fears that ever since he was a tiny *enfant*, back in Trois Rivieres. Once, when we fight the Peigan, I was hide in a small cave and the roof fell in. Black? I tell you . . . it was so black in there I could not see my own hand. I was so scared, I burst out of that cave like an old bear in the springtime, roaring and screaming like I am insane. Those Peigan, they got so scared they all ran away, and everybody thought old René was a hero. Humph! I was more afraid of the dark in that cave than those damned Peigan were scared of me, but I don't ever tell anybody that."

René paused abruptly, staring not quite at Garth, but over his shoulder. His voice softened as he whispered, "Behind you, on the ridge, there is a fat mountain goat. The noise you make is not important now, so go and shoot him, *s'il vous plaît,* and we will have fresh meat, at least, while we decide what next to do."

An hour later, they were sprawled beside a dying fire, replete with tasty roast goat meat and feeling marginally better about the whole situation. René had taken up Savard's back trail and determined that he'd been alone when ambushing them.

"It makes little sense," he said. "Unless he needed the horses for some reason, but that doesn't explain where the other of his weasels is, or the girl. Come, finish up your meal and let us pack up more meat for the trail, which I fear will be a long one. We will be slower than him on these mountain trails, unless the horse he stole gives out quickly. With a stone bruise one can never tell, and we might get lucky."

Chapter Ten

Lucien Cardinal was a poor woodsman. It was the fourth day since he'd fled with the girl and the last two days had been horrors of wind and rain and blackflies. Cardinal had been raised in the buffalo grass country of the prairies, and the shining Rocky Mountains were as foreign to him as some hostile eastern city. He not only feared the dark, shadowy woodlands; he was hopelessly inept when it came to traveling there.

Instead of sticking to the ridge trails frequented by the mountain caribou and elk, he'd started seeking shortcuts along moose trails through the myriads of muskeg meadows, where the sloppy footing and hordes of savage insects had taken their toll on the ponies' strength.

Lucien would gladly have turned back to the south but for his fear of Savard and the possibility of Garth and René having picked up his trail. As it was, he couldn't pick up his own back trail and ended up wandering in an erratic course toward the Athabasca, driving Ilona's pony ahead of his own because he'd lost the leading line.

At mid-morning, they crested a low ridge and saw, in the distance below, the dark, broad swiftness of the Athabasca River, with a smaller and clearer stream joining it. Behind them, the clouds were breaking, and there was some indication the skies might clear.

Cardinal pushed Ilona's pony ahead of him down the ridge on trails that no sane rider would have attempted. Only Ilona's superior horsemanship saved her from several serious falls. Cardinal whipped his own mount along behind hers, at one point stopping only inches from plunging all of them over a steep cliff and into the surging torrent. After much scrambling over deadfall timber and through mushy riverbank springs, they gained a wide sandbar, where he directed Ilona to set up camp.

The relative openness of the Athabasca valley pleased him, as did the unwary mule deer doe that wandered within musket shot a few moments later. Not trusting Ilona with his knife, he dressed out the animal himself, then dragged it to the edge of the makeshift camp and directed Ilona to cook the succulent steaks he slashed from the hindquarter.

Once they'd eaten—she with hands still bound in front of her—Cardinal tied Ilona securely to a nearby tree, then slipped away to scout for sign of passing Indians or parties of voyageurs on the river. In hindsight, he wished he'd not used the musket, although the muffled noise it made was less than a rifle might have created. But still . . .

Ilona had almost worked free of her bonds when Cardinal returned, unexpectedly, from the opposite direction he'd taken when leaving the camp. It had been an arduous effort to stretch against her tether until she could extend her wrists and reach a tiny pool, but the effect—if slow—was significant. Once the rawhide thongs were moistened, they became slimy and could be stretched if she exerted all her strength. But not quite stretched enough to free her. Cardinal, preoccupied when he returned, didn't seem to notice, and she had renewed hopes that she might free herself during the dark of the coming night.

But her wishes went awry when eventually he inspected the bonds, cursing when he discovered her endeavors.

"Bitch!" he snarled, then kicked her over on her side and sat on her while he yanked the wet rawhide tighter. But his mind was elsewhere. He'd scouted near the junction of the two streams, finding a well-used pony trail he thought might take them away from the mountains and eastward to the open prairies he so hoped now to find. His limited knowledge of the region was based purely upon hearsay, but he was convinced they had found the Athabasca River and could find a relatively easy way out of the mountains by heading downstream.

His security renewed, Lucien slashed off a fresh steak from the deer carcass, broiled it over the flames, then proceeded to gorge himself. With scarcely a glance at Ilona, he curled up on the sun-warmed sand and was noisily asleep in moments.

His snoring was Ilona's clue to renew her attempts to stretch the rawhide, now drying so tight her hands were turning an ugly, dark hue from lack of circulation. For two hours, she patiently twisted and turned her wrists, ignoring the pain. She couldn't gain enough slack in the rawhide to free herself, but at least she could manage enough to restore her circulation.

Eventually, exhaustion and the warm breeze took their toll, and she, too, dozed in the sunshine. Except it was not a peaceful sleep. Her mind leapt and raced through a succession of tormented dreams . . .

. . . *always she was running. As a child through the high buffalo grass, then as a young woman, bounding through forests and swamps in the mountain foothills. Behind her, a monstrous, bear-like creature, sometimes with the shaggy, bearded pig-face of Savard and sometimes with the crafty, weasel features of the Cardinal brothers.*

Usually, she was naked, her graceful legs a welter of fly bites and bramble cuts. And often she stumbled and fell, rolling in frantic fear through nettle patches and alder thickets. And always the beast man—or men—were close behind, threatening to kill her, eat her, or worse. She was not afraid of her nakedness, not ashamed of it, but her instincts screamed at the inability to cleanse her cuts and bites, or rest her weary legs . . .

Her own moans awoke her from the torment of writhing and groveling to escape the itching fly bites of her dreams. Her arms were numb to the elbows because the drying rawhide had again threatened the circulation, and her knee-length tunic had worked itself up around her waist during her dream contortions.

Ilona struggled to her knees and turned to find the cold, bright eyes of Lucien Cardinal leering fixedly at her. She needed no guidebook to read his thoughts, and her father's advice sprang to mind.

"Rape," he had said, "may someday be inevitable. This is a harsh land, and such is a fact of life. What you must remember is that most men who would rape a woman—even amongst the Indians—have little or no confidence in their ability to win her affections any other way. That does not apply to one like Savard, of course. He is simply a cruel and brutal man . . . a sick man, really . . . and the pleasure he would take from a woman would be based on the fear and torment he could inflict. No coy tricks would put him off, but it may be possible with some other men to use an appeal to their better nature, at least to try and buy yourself more time."

On that particular occasion, his advice had seemed vaguely irrelevant, but one look at Lucien Cardinal brought each word alive in her memory. She could hear her father speak and understood her captor only too well. Apart from her brief attack upon Elzear, Ilona's approach to her captivity had been typically Indian. She had maintained a stoic, submissive silence, done precisely what she was told, and done her best to avoid notice.

She could see, however, where such docility with Lucien Cardinal might prove her downfall. So she resolved to use whatever feminine wiles she possessed in an attempt to stave off his violence, perhaps even outwit him and somehow escape. She no longer had any hope that Garth and René might rescue her, but in the deep woodlands of the mountain foothills she knew herself to be more than a match for the prairie-raised half-breed Cardinal. All she needed was a decent head start and a bit of luck. Surviving this night unscathed would be a nice start.

He was no leader, she reasoned. With him, boldness might succeed where a meek approach would only hasten his ill use of her.

"If you would untie me, I could cook us a decent meal," she murmured softly in Cree. "There is really no need to keep me tied up like this. I can't go anywhere, after all. And besides, it hurts my arms. Look, my hands are turning black. I'll be no good to you if my fingers fall off."

Cardinal seemed visibly startled by her words, the first she had spoken directly to him since her capture at Acton House.

"What kind of trick is this, *Mooniaskwew*?" he snarled, baring his teeth like the weasel he so resembled.

"I am no white woman," she retorted. "You know my father, and you know my mother is of the south Peigan. I am as much Indian as you."

"Then why does the red-haired young white man chase after you? White men don't chase after Indian women. They buy them. I think you are trying to trick me in some way."

"Why should I want to trick you? You saved me from that pig Savard, didn't you? I hope the *okistgutowan*—the grizzly bear—ate him alive. *Muchi-manitowiw!* He is an evil man . . . a devil!"

Lucien appeared confused and uneasy in the face of her directness, but his eyes seemed to confirm how her hands were turning black because her lashings were too tight. And one thing was obvious: where could she go?

"All right. I'll untie you. But one trick and I will cut your heart out and eat it raw. Do you understand?"

Ilona nodded demurely and, once freed, competently began

to put together the makings of a real feast: broiled ribs, tenderloin baked in the coals, and liver sprinkled with gall to increase the flavor. Lucien, at least partly taken in by her apparent complicity, lay back beside the fire and concerned himself with whetting his knife blade; although not, Ilona noticed, without keeping a watchful eye on her every move. But he appeared to have forgotten—at least for the moment—his lust.

That security was short-lived, however. Immediately after they had eaten, he began to question her, using extremely crude expletives in both Cree and his English *patois*, clearly to turn the conversation to sexual matters.

How old was she . . . and had she known many men? But, of course, none. It was plain, he ventured, that she must be a maiden of the highest desirability. But the young white man from Rocky Mountain House? Surely he would not chase after a woman of mixed blood without some . . . expectations? Had he perhaps brought ponies to her father's lodge? Was he negotiating to buy her, maybe?

Ilona found herself confused by the weasel's swift, sly, probing questions. She had planned to use words as weapons but now was finding them poor defenders. The more Cardinal talked, the more she noticed a bright glow of lust kindling behind his narrow, probing eyes. More importantly, she was running out of answers. Each time she attempted to steer the conversation to safer ground, he parried her words.

And he was moving closer to her with virtually every comment, obviously aware that even untied she could do little to escape him. He had left her hands unbound, but he made sure he was always positioned between Ilona and the ponies.

Eventually, his queries became bluntly specific.

"Look at me. Am I not a desirable man in your eyes? Truly, I am but thirty winters old, and I am well-formed, am I not? Surely not a hulking bear like that Savard, who would not waste words with you. Be glad it is I, Lucien Cardinal, that you are with, or you would already be well used by Savard. He would not waste all this time on idle talk."

Cardinal's voice grew thick with lust, and he offered her a sickly, evil smile as his fingers fumbled with his breech-clout. "Come closer, little Climbing Woman," he said softly. "I will give you something to climb. Is that not a good joke? Do not be afraid of Lucien. I will not harm you, provided you are a good girl, of course, and not a nuisance.

"I have had a white woman, too, you know. At Trois Rivieres, it was. She was the daughter of a shopkeeper there, and much sought after by all the white men in the town. But she looked at Lucien Cardinal, and she knew a real man when she saw one. In the grass behind her father's store, I took her one night. She screamed, but they were screams of pleasure."

Ilona knew even as he reached for her that the talking was finished, but hope fluttered that she would be able to summon up some words that might stop him. Then he put one greasy hand on her wrist, and she instinctively recoiled, stammering for useful words as she evaded his touch.

Lucien leapt to his feet, clawing aside the breech-clout to reveal a startling erection.

"Hah! Here is a pole for the Climbing Woman," he snarled. "And you *will* climb it, you half-white slut. You try to tell Lucien Cardinal that you are Peigan. If that were truly so, you would have begged for this days ago."

Throwing his weight upon her, Lucien tried to hold her down while he thrust under her tunic with one hand. Ilona writhed and struggled, but inexorably the man's superior weight and strength began to prevail. She attempted to knee him in the groin, but he easily countered the move, and retaliated by clouting her across the face with his free hand.

"Slut," he growled. "Be still or I will break your face. You will like it what I am going to do with you. Tomorrow you will be crying for more, I tell you that."

His second blow almost drove her to unconsciousness, but suddenly he was lifted up off her, and she saw him fly through the air to land with a thud on the other side of the fire.

"Stinking half-breed dog. I will teach you not to betray Louis Savard," roared the savage apparition that arose in the firelight. He loomed like an ogre in the half light, appearing even larger than life. He had slunk into the camp unnoticed, and now he'd gained the advantage.

Lucien's knife had gone flying when Savard threw him across the fire and into the shadows. Savard thrust his own knife back into its sheath, muttering, "Take it if you can, little weasel. I've killed better men than you with my bare hands."

Leaping across the fire, he grabbed for Lucien, who dodged back into the darkness of the underbrush, looking for a place to run. Ilona, quick to see the possibility of her own escape, edged into the shadows behind her, instinctively moving towards the horses. Then, realizing a whinny of alarm would only serve to alert her tormentors, she chose instead to try and make it to the river, hoping she might slip in unnoticed and swim quietly downstream with the current, perhaps even cross to the other side.

Behind her, the sounds of combat told their story. Savard was deliberately taunting the smaller half-breed. Savard was obviously secure in his own bear-like strength. He apparently took particular pleasure in baiting and taunting the smaller man. From Savard's words, she knew he could read the fear in Lucien Cardinal's eyes as Savard closed in on him.

"Come, little man. Do not run away from Louis Savard. Fight. I am only going to break your little weasel bones, one by one. You had such a hard-on for the little *Peigan* slut . . . show it to me and I shall break that bone first. And then feed it to you.

"What's the matter, little half-breed bastard? Are you afraid? Come here, into my arms. I'll treat you as gently as that little white-skinned bitch. Come into my arms . . . and die."

The sounds faded as Ilona reached the riverbank and slid into the icy mountain waters as quietly as any otter. But otters have fur and stay warm even when swimming. By the time she reached the far shore and staggered onto a hard-packed sandbar . . . far downstream from where she'd gone in . . . she was so chilled she could barely think, barely walk, never mind run.

But her mind raced in a frenzy of planning. She must hide, but where? How? In the darkness it was impossible to travel without leaving sign. In the pale moonlight, she crossed the narrow bar and realized she was at the junction where a smaller stream intersected with the mighty Athabasca. Immediately she knew where her best chance was, and she turned upstream in the smaller waterway, shuddering with the cold, but able to wade from gravel bar to gravel bar, seldom in water more than waist deep. If she didn't freeze to death first, she thought, there might yet be hope.

The moon gave her little assistance, but there was enough light to let her distinguish sand from water, shadow from grasping, clutching willow branch. The bottom was mostly fine gravel, but in places the gravel was coarser, and there wasn't enough light to guide her. She had to use her own stature in the water as a guide, stepping ahead gingerly and putting her feet down with care so as not to hurt herself. Her moccasins, once soaked, gave her little protection from the stones, and her buckskin tunic and leggings provided no warmth.

Teeth chattering so loudly she half feared that sound alone might betray her, she managed almost a mile of trackless travel before exhaustion made further progress impossible. Shaking with the chill, unsure if she could survive without the fire she dared not make even had she been able to, she scrambled her way under a deadfall spruce and curled up in a pile of fallen needles, gathering them around her and piling them on top of her until exhaustion won out, and she slipped into unconsciousness.

CHAPTER ELEVEN

The broken body of Lucien Cardinal was mute evidence of the tortures Savard had inflicted. Garth and René stood with the horse for several moments before moving in to look closely at the corpse.

"*Mon Dieu!* The man must be truly mad," said René. "Look at this. Every finger broken. Almost every bone in the whole body, also. I fear we follow a madman, *mon ami.*"

Garth shuddered at the sight. From the expression on Cardinal's face, he'd been alive through most of the torture, and Garth could see all too well in his own mind Savard's activities and the inherent evil of it all.

"Good Christ, René, what kind of animal is he? This wasn't a fight; it was pure and simple torture. This poor son-of-a-bitch never had a chance to even defend himself."

René, meanwhile, had been scouting the fringe of the campsite, and he rose from his careful scrutiny of the ground to curse in his excitement. "*Sacré!* He's not got the girl with him. Look at these tracks: only one horse of the three has a rider, and I am sure it is Savard, himself. Where did she go, I wonder? She was here . . . that much is for certain."

The small voyageur spat in disgust. "And just as bad, the bastard didn't leave us even one of those horses! It is going to be a long walk out of here, *mon ami*. This nag cannot carry double for much further. He has enough merely to carry you."

"Well, if we were both your size, little monkey, we'd need

only half a horse," Garth replied with a grim laugh. "And there's nothing to be done about it for now, anyway. Let us check these tracks some more. Maybe we can figure out where the girl went, because without a horse, she can't have gone far. Unless she went into the river."

"That is where Cardinal is going, too. Here, give me a hand with the poor bastard and we will let the river bury him. If this is the Athabasca, and I think it must be, he will make good food for the giant fish the Indians say live in these waters."

As they dragged Cardinal's body to the edge of the sandbar, René almost immediately spotted where Ilona had gone into the water, but it took them three hours of patient searching—after they had found a place to swim the horse and themselves across—for his keen eyes to spot the tiny signs of her diversion into the smaller stream that joined the Athabasca. Garth would have scoffed at the old man's certainty if he hadn't—through past experience—become convinced of René's phenomenal tracking abilities.

To Garth's eyes, what René pointed out looked like nothing at all, and surely not the mark of Ilona's heel as she had stepped to the sand to avoid a huge tree lying across the current. But that single, tiny clue was sufficient for René to move on and find others, confirming his suggestion that she had gone upstream, away from the main river.

"She is smart, this one," he told Garth. "And she is moving pretty fast, too. If she sticks to this small river, we can maybe catch up by taking shortcuts, but I am afraid we might pass her in the night or some such thing. She is only one day ahead of us, now, but if we have to slow down too much in the tracking, she will gain on that.

"I think it is best that you take the horse and scout ahead for maybe two, three days, my friend. Maybe you can get ahead of her and leave some signs so she can find us, or at least know we are here and searching for her. But don't forget this girl has been through some bad times. She is going to run from any man she sees, I'm thinking. Maybe she won't even trust you and me.

"And watch out for Savard! I think from his track he has gone on down the Athabasca on the other side, but maybe it is only a trick, and he is out there ahead someplace. If you see him, you could ask him nicely if he'll lend us a horse . . . no?"

The little man's backhanded humor didn't detract from the seriousness in his voice, and Garth knew there was indeed a good chance of Savard being ahead of them, searching for Ilona as they were, and unquestionably dangerous.

"If I see him, I'll ask him, all right, soon as I shoot the bastard full of holes," Garth replied in a grim voice. "I'll leave your blankets and some food on one of the gravel bars up ahead, so you won't have to carry them. And I will leave enough sign so you can know what I am up to."

"Do not leave them too far ahead," René replied. "Remember that tracking is slow travel, and besides, I am an old man. I cannot move so fast anymore."

Three days later, having seen no sign of the missing girl or anyone else, Garth was sprawled on a high cut bank, peering cautiously at the valley below him, when he saw a brief, bright flash of movement. He had chosen this spot because it gave him an unobstructed view of the river valley, and now was glad of his choice.

Dropping further into cover amidst some low alders, he concentrated his gaze on the spot where he'd seen the movement. At the same time, he quietly cocked his rifle. A moment later, old René stepped cautiously out from cover, and Garth sprang to his feet, waving. But René, peering along his own back trail and then up towards Garth, gave no indication he'd seen the younger man. Garth stuck two fingers in his mouth, all prepared to whistle, but a quick gesture from his old friend sent him immediately down into hiding again.

René slid away into cover, and it was nearly an hour later when he panted to the crest beside Garth, arriving from the opposite side of the ridge.

"*Mon Dieu,* but I am getting old," he whispered in a voice hoarse with exertion. "I must lie down now and rest, or I will for certain die. You sneak back to where you can see the flats where I was coming out. I am not sure, but I think somebody, he's following me. Maybe Savard. Maybe even the girl. I am not sure.

"That girl, she is good in the bush! I find only a few signs where she has come ashore to pick berries, and once where she knocked down a foolish grouse with a stick. And tough! A white woman—and most men, too—would have died already in this jungle. It is a nightmare to travel. But the girl, she has eaten the grouse raw, and she don't stop moving, not for anything. It might be she is moving quickly to try and stay warm; that water is like ice and it must be hard for her.

"She might even be ahead of us yet, but somebody is follow old René, and this time it should be us who lay the trap. Not like the last time, eh? I have been shot at enough on this trip, me."

An hour's fruitless vigilance took a toll on Garth's patience, and he was about ready to give it up when he saw a pony stick its nose out of the brush where René had first emerged. He was half turned to alert his companion when he felt René's hand on his arm.

"It is as I thought—that half-breed bastard Savard. Look at the face on that horse. It is for sure that runty little roan. There could not be two such ugly horses in the entire world," René whispered.

"What you must do is guard that trail up the bluff," he continued. "See how that pony holds his head? He is tied up there, and I think Savard is trying to sneak up this way on foot while the horse, he distracts us. Maybe it is time he learned a trick or two from old René. You guard the trail and our one horse. I am going to sneak around the other side of this little river and try to separate Savard from that little roan. Such an ugly little horse, but even that one is better than none. And I am tired of walking, *non?*"

The little horse didn't move for a full hour, nor did anything else along the bluff's sharp edge. Garth was becoming worried and impatient when a shot rang out, startling both him and the pony he guarded. He lost a moment grabbing for its halter rope when it attempted to bolt, and when the horse had been properly secured, he was about to plunge down the trail when René came out of the brush, cantering along on Savard's little roan pony.

Moments later, the small voyageur arrived on the bluff with a broad smile on his ugly face, and humming a bawdy French river tune.

"Ho! You can see, *mon ami,* that we are both now horsemen again, and Savard, he is going to have a headache for a few days, I think. But I must check the sights on this weapon. Ah, such a shame to miss a lovely target like that at only two hundred yards.

"*Mon Dieu,* I show that big bear he isn't the only woodsman in the country. I could have stolen that pony right from under his nose, but Savard, he made such a good target I could not resist to take only the one shot at him. An inch lower, by God, and he would be a dead pig.

"He is one smart son-of-a-bitch, that one. He tied that pony up as bait, for sure. I do not know how he figured out we were up here, but he was curled up under a deadfall, waiting for us to come down that far trail. Ah . . . such a shot to have missed! But all I did was crease his brow a little. A gentle caress, but not enough to damage that thick skull. And he had the other two ponies tied up where he was hiding, so all I could grab was this one."

René laughed. "You should have seen that big bear run! He was on a horse and into the timber so fast I couldn't hope to reload for a second shot. But at least René, he doesn't have to walk anymore. Little ugly one, you are the most beautiful ugly horse in all the world—for now, anyway."

"Well, old man, I'm glad to see that pony myself, but I surely wish you'd done more serious damage to that bastard Savard. He may be running now, but we've not seen the last of him. Now that he is sure where we are, he'll be like a deer tick on our trail. And what of the signs I left for you along the river? Any indication Ilona might have seen them?"

"*Non.* I'm pretty sure you never caught up with her. She travels in the river like an otter, that one, and now she will have heard that shot and will be even more careful. And we must guard our backs, which will slow us down. You are right about Savard. He will not give up. But now he sees old René is not so stupid, he will travel maybe a little slower, more cautiously."

"Well I think we should stop jawing and try to make a mile. You may have frightened Savard, but it won't last for long, and I'd rather have him behind us than ahead, so let us get going, old man."

They booted their ponies down the bluff and headed off again upriver, determined to use speed in a bid to catch the fleeing girl. If nothing else, it now seemed likely she would keep to the stream, having done so for this long.

CHAPTER TWELVE

Ilona watched from a ridge-top thicket as Garth and René rode into the small Cree camp of Sleeping Elk and his band. Half dead from exhaustion, hunger, and the icy waters of the river, she'd been lying there almost a full day, trying to summon the strength and courage to approach the camp.

In a semi-delirious state from the blackfly bites that covered her body and the hunger that kept her weak, Ilona was certain she'd recognized many of the Cree, except that their images seemed to change with every gasping breath. One stooped, older squaw had appeared as Ilona's own mother, and the girl had almost run out into the open. But then her mind saw Savard's hulking figure amongst the warriors, and she'd sunk deeper into the thicket, shuddering with fear.

The sound of Garth's booming voice brought renewed hope and confidence. None of the visions she had seen had spoken. Surely there could be no mistaking that voice, her mind assured her, and she rose, was about to step into the open and run to him, when a hand grasped her from behind, and she was yanked backwards and dragged to the ground.

Twisting to free herself, although too weak to do much, she got a good look at her captor, opened her mouth to scream . . . then fainted dead away.

Nothing in Ilona's young life had prepared her for the face of Mad Wolf. It was a grinning, toothless skull, covered in wrinkled leather, and the eyes were like running sores.

The old Cree was aptly named. He had survived smallpox but was slowly losing the battle with advanced syphilis and was half blind and seriously demented. He'd been cast out of almost every Cree band along the northern foothills for his vicious attacks on children and young girls, but superstition had kept the tribes from killing him outright, so he lurked on the outskirts of any camp that would allow it, like some hideously sub-human camp scavenger.

There had been three incidents in Sleeping Elk's camp, but not until the chief's own daughter had been threatened was the aging madman ordered away. With him had gone the old, lame widow, Calling Loon. She was no longer of any use to the band, and had no relatives to care for her since her only son had died in a battle with a Blackfoot raiding party.

Mad Wolf had gladly taken up with the old woman. In his own delusions, he fancied himself a great war chief, and therefore entitled to slaves. He and Calling Loon had spent the summer on the shores of nearby Rock Lake, scavenging for carrion and eating anything they could find.

The old man had been scouting Sleeping Elk's camp with a view to stealing food and supplies to face the coming winter when he'd spotted Ilona spying from the thicket. In the old man's warped mind, she was merely another potential slave, although her fainting confused him slightly. Still, he gathered the unconscious girl in his arms and fled back to his own camp, where he left Ilona to the attentions of Calling Loon and returned to his original mission.

He, too, had witnessed the arrival of Garth and René and interpreted the rare sight of white men as good omens for his own plans. At worst, he thought in a rare moment of clarity, it would distract the people of Sleeping Elk's band and provide him a better than usual chance to steal whatever he might find.

Sleeping Elk was less than pleased by the visit of the white travelers. His band was an offshoot of the Sunchild Cree, and he had been drifting steadily north along the foothills for several years in a deliberate attempt to avoid contact with the whites.

His disenchantment dated back to his first meeting with the pale strangers, at one of the earliest Hudson's Bay Company posts ever established in the south-central foothills of the mountains. Using liberal draughts of trade rum, the traders had cunningly separated Sleeping Elk's people from furs needed for the coming winter—a harsh one that year—and then cheated the Cree out of their best horses.

He greeted these two new riders, therefore, with no more manners or welcome than Indian tradition demanded. It was only René's fluent use of the Cree language that gained them permission to rest in the camp. Once René had explained the purpose of their journey, Sleeping Elk's suspicions dulled slightly, but he nonetheless resolved to watch them closely during their visit.

With their horses turned out into the village pony herd and their gear stowed in the chief's lodge, Garth and René set out to explore the camp and see if anyone had knowledge of the girl they were seeking. Their enquiries amongst the hunters met with such open hostility, however, that they soon abandoned the effort and retired to Sleeping Elk's lodge to rest until dinner.

The chief had decreed that no special feast would be held for the white visitors and, instead, invited them to share his own meal. A huge cauldron filled with braised ribs and moose nose stew had been simmering throughout the afternoon. The invitation caused René to jest—in English—"I am glad, me, that we are not guests. This is wonderful, and better than dog meat, I'm thinking."

Garth grinned cheerfully, dipping into the pot for another

chunk of the tender, strong-flavored meat. "How do you know this isn't dog, little one? Sure as hell I couldn't tell the difference."

"Ah, the dog would be even more tender. I have eaten it many times in the southern camps, especially amongst the Peigan. The thing I don't like is that they don't bother to gut the puppies before they are cooked. They just singe off some of the hair and dump them into the pot. This is much better."

A sullen grunt from the chief ended the conversation abruptly. "He does not like us to speak what he cannot understand," explained René, pointing to Garth and addressing Sleeping Elk in a rattle of guttural Cree that Garth couldn't follow.

After the meal, René and the chief got involved in a lengthy dissertation in Cree, which left Garth with little to do. He spread his blankets against the back edge of the teepee, curled up in them, and dropped off to sleep. Hours, it seemed, had passed by the time old René joined him and the camp drifted into a stillness penetrated only by the occasional barking of a dog.

The dogs didn't bark at Mad Wolf. They could smell him coming from half a mile away, but his odor was essentially Cree, vaguely familiar, and they paid little attention. One dog snapped at him as he skulked past the teepee of Two Arrows, but a flying kick discouraged further attack.

He was passing the back of Sleeping Elk's lodge when he saw a knife handle sticking out beneath the teepee skirt. Chuckling softly, he scooped it up and continued down the line of silent lodges.

A musket, several moose-hide garments, and a cooking pot later, he was trying to dislodge a fine war bow from its lashings on the owner's teepee when a grunt from within halted him. Mad Wolf slipped behind the partially opened teepee flap, the newfound knife ready in his hand. When the flap bulged outward, he drove the knife deep into the emerging warrior, stabbed three times more, then fled when the knife caught on some internal barrier.

Walks-With-Horses died silently. Only the slightest of groans escaped his lips as he crumpled in the entranceway, and his young wife paid no attention to the sound, didn't notice him fall. Not until the light of dawn did she waken the camp with her shrill screams of anguish.

One faction of Sleeping Elk's warriors would have killed Garth and René immediately after Walks-With-Horses was found with Garth's easily recognized knife joining his belly to the collapsed teepee flap. But the old chief refused to believe the young white man could have left his own lodge, killed Walks-With-Horses, and returned without being caught.

"Am I a woman, that you think I could sleep so soundly?" he shouted at the raging warriors. "Clearly, this young white man did not kill Walks-With-Horses, but it cannot be denied these men have brought bad medicine with them, and perhaps even some evil spirits that killed our friend. They will leave us, but they came in peace and will leave the same way. I have spoken."

He personally guided the two men to the edge of the camp and made it clear there would be no second chances, turning his back on their departure almost immediately.

"It was that bastard Savard," Garth hissed, his voice sibilant against the rumble of disgruntled voices from behind them. "There's no other explanation I can think of."

"Never mind the explanations. We must ride, and ride fast, I'm thinking," replied René. "Did you not see the look on the face of the dead one's brother? The chief, he has let us go to save face for himself, but for sure there will be some of those warriors trying to take our hair before we leave their country."

"But what about Ilona? She can't be all that far from this area."

"She is not in that camp, for sure. I think she is probably dead, her. But if not, she is ahead of us still. Come this way. We have gone south long enough. Now we must swing around the valley and head north again. Maybe that will fool these young bucks enough to give us a few days more to search."

Garth followed as René led the way through a convoluted procedure of walking in the nearby stream, then turning to return past their entry point and out of the water onto a rock ledge that would show no tracks.

"Damn that Savard. It would have been a good camp in which to winter, that one," the old man said. "They have lost enough warriors to the Blackfoot that there are lots of young widows there who will be cold when the snow comes. Me, I'm beginning to think the old chief was right. There's bad medicine involved with this trip."

Chapter Thirteen

Bull's Brother led the six young Indians who caught up with Garth and René at Sheep Creek. He was the first to die. Three others died before the remaining pair decided there was too much risk in their pursuit of the fleeing white men.

Had they persisted, thought Garth, success would have been more likely than failure.

René had taken a musket ball high in his right shoulder, pressing against the shoulder blade. The bleeding was minimal, and he told Garth the shoulder wasn't broken, but his effectiveness in the fight had abruptly ended.

Garth had taken two wounds, both minor. A ball had passed through his left calf but missed bone and major blood vessels. His other wound was a slice across one bicep from a passing arrow.

René was in tremendous pain but insisted they should first seek out a decent hiding place, and only then worry about their wounds.

"We do not know how many more of those Cree there are on the trail," he muttered through clenched teeth. "Those two who escaped, even, might once again decide to be brave, and they might be too much for you to handle alone. Me, I am not going to be much help."

They splashed in and out of the creek for about six miles, taking every precaution to hide their tracks, before finding a campsite René would approve. By then, his wrinkled face was ashen, and it was all he could do to sit his pony.

Garth carried his old friend down off the horse, gently placing him on a blanket in a dry spot beneath a spreading pine tree. Then he washed the wound with chilled creek water. The danger of infection, he knew, was far more real than any harm the ball itself might have caused. There was no great loss of blood, but the wound was already becoming inflamed.

"The ball, it must come out," gasped René, almost faint with the effort of speaking.

"But how? I am no doctor, and I have no tools for such a thing. I'm not about to start slicing you up with a six-inch skinning knife, old friend."

"Old *dead* friend if you do not," was the reply. "The ball, it is resting on the shoulder blade. What you must do is cut me open at the back and push the ball through, over the back, with a stick or something. It must come out, young Cameron. That Indian lead is always dirty, and the wound will poison me for certain if we do not get it out. I cannot help you. The pain, it is too much . . ." He mumbled a few more words in French, then lapsed into unconsciousness.

Faced with the responsibility, Garth put together the smallest fire possible, heated some water to boiling, and set to work. Plunging his knife into the white-hot coals and then into the boiling water, he felt along René's shoulder to the darkening lump he presumed must be the musket ball.

The first cut, in his attempt to inflict no more pain than absolutely needed, was useless—it barely broke the skin. The second was better, but he didn't think it deep enough to reach the musket ball. In any event, he couldn't get purchase so as to move it.

In desperation, he scrubbed down his ramrod, steeled himself for the effort, and thrust it into the wound. It grated once on bone, forcing an involuntary groan from René, but Garth was able to push the musket ball back along its original track until he could flick it free with the knife point.

The old man's back and shoulder were slick with blood from Garth's butchery, so he bathed the infected area again with hot water, then with cold, in an attempt to staunch the bleeding. Then he plugged the holes with compresses of boiled caribou moss, bound the shoulder with his remaining relatively clean rag, and let the old man rest.

The next four days were torture for both men, but Garth perhaps suffered the worst because he was aware of the problems. René's wound had become badly infected—hardly any surprise—and he was feverish, thrusting his body around in convulsions, and moaning and raving in French. But he never properly regained consciousness, which Garth thought was a blessing, much as he would have welcomed the old man's forest skills and knowledge.

René's entire shoulder was black with bad blood and swollen to grotesque proportions. Garth was in a mental frenzy. He didn't know what he'd done wrong and had only the vaguest idea of how to help his old friend.

Reasoning that René would die, anyway, if he didn't do some damned thing, he slashed a green alder shoot to a razor-sharp point and drove it entirely through the wound with a single blow from his knife-hilt. The action released a huge gout of blood and evil-smelling pus but at least left him with a vague idea of how he might cleanse the inside of the wound.

With little to lose at this point, he propped the unconscious voyageur over a log, held the entrance to the injury open with the alder stick, and poured scalding water right through the gaping wound . . . over and over until it ran more or less clear and clean.

René's fever broke during the night, and by late the next day he could speak in a voice that was weak, but coherent.

"I am afraid to even ask what you have done to me, my friend. I know of a certainty that I am not dead; there is too much pain for that. But the way I feel, maybe death might be better, *non*?"

He listened to Garth's explanations, felt gingerly of the injured shoulder, then issued a lengthy list of commands, his voice growing miraculously stronger as his natural leadership began to re-emerge.

"Meat! That is what we must have . . . and soon. Do not worry about me, for now. Go out and kill the first deer or moose or elk you find, or even a rabbit, but preferably deer or moose. And when you come back, bring first the liver. Part of it you must put on the wound to draw the remaining poison, but the rest you must hang in a tree to draw flies and make maggots.

"It is the dead flesh inside that is still poisoning me, and you cannot reach all of it inside that enormous tunnel you have made in my shoulder. The maggots can do that, if the poison has not spread too far."

For once, luck was in their favor. Garth dropped a large mule deer buck within half a mile of the camp and was back with the steaming liver before an hour had passed. René had once again slipped into unconsciousness, albeit without the fever, so Garth opened the dressings and applied the warm liver to both sides of the wound. Then he hung a large piece in a tree some distance down-wind from camp, thinking idly it would be equally good bait for any passing grizzly bear, which would be about the final straw in their current predicament.

A few days was all it took to grow a thriving crop of maggots, and they, in turn, took a similar time to cleanse René's wound to the point where proper healing was noticeable. A hearty diet of the rich venison, first in broth form and then in roasts and chops, restored René to a measure of his former self within a week, although he still had to admit considerable weakness.

Within another week, they were headed south, against Garth's wishes but in keeping with the older man's unarguable logic.

"Listen, my friend. There is no further need to search for the girl. She is not with Savard. She is not in the camp of Sleeping Elk . . . not that we could go back and search there again . . . and she is not with us. Even a tough, forest-wise young one like her would not have survived this long in the wilderness alone, with no weapons, no tools, no knowledge of where she even is. *C'est impossible.*

"Now, we will go back south, us. If we can slip around the camp of the Cree without another fight, and if we hurry, and if we are luckier than we have been, we may even be home again before the deep snows, they come. Which they will!"

Accepting the sorrow on his young friend's face, René softened his remarks. "But we will move slowly, and old René will keep a sharp eye out all the way, and I promise you, if we find even the smallest sign of the girl, we will turn around again and look for her. I, René, promise you this!"

René's dreams of a pleasant, idle winter back at Rocky Mountain House on the North Saskatchewan were short-lived. They continued travelling close to water, as Garth insisted, and three days along, René crested a low rise and dismounted to stalk silently along the stream-side in search of a suitably secluded campsite.

"*C'est impossible,*" he cried. "I could have sworn that girl could not be still alive, but, Garth, come and look at this! Unless I am going crazy, me, here are tracks from that Ilona's moccasins."

He continued speaking even as Garth leapt from his own pony in a rush to join the old woodsman. "It must be so. They are of the right size, and of the Blackfoot design, and they are so tattered, it must be her! I do not understand this at all. This

is not a camp of Savard's. There have been three people here
. . . the girl, an old woman, a *lame* old woman—and a man.
They are Cree, from their moccasin tracks, but why then are
they not with old Sleeping Elk?"

Garth and René followed the sign for two silent days. René
seldom spoke, intent upon trying to unravel the story left by the
few tracks he could find. Garth was delegated to scout out to
the sides, keeping a sharp eye out for any ambush, but warned
specifically not to let his pony step where it might disturb the
tracks René was so diligently trying to follow.

Late on the second day, the old voyageur was muttering
constantly to himself in gutter French, shaking his head and
coursing back and forth like a dog seeking fresh scent. Then he
stopped his pony in a sheltered glade and began to speak in a
rapid conglomeration of oaths and instructions.

"*Sacré bleu!* It is enough. We are going to stop here, and old
René, he is going to rest his useless eyes for a time. *Mère de
Dieu.* I cannot understand what is taking place. Now it is two
horses we are trailing, but the girl walks . . . always, she walks.
And I do not know why this is, but I am almost certain she is
tied to the tail of one horse. What is going on here, I do not
know.

"For an entire day, now, there has been no sign of the lame
one, the old woman. What has she done? Grown wings like the
bird and flown away? The whole trail, it makes no sense. This
man does not know where he is going, I am thinking. Or else he
knows he is being followed. *Mon Dieu.* I cannot tell."

Garth, both amused by his companion's antics and confused
by the ravings, could only shake his own head and begin making up the temporary camp as René directed. Even after dinner,
when the old man had calmed down enough to explain the
problem more thoroughly, Garth still couldn't quite believe so
much could be read from so few scattered tracks.

"René is right, you will see, if we ever catch up to these people. But their trail, it is nearly impossible to follow, and I fear they are gaining on us each day. So tomorrow, we shall split up. You will ride well to the side, but quickly, and far ahead. Follow the most logical route, but be careful of any ambush. I will follow the tracks as I find them, since this old man we follow is a foxy one, and I am not sure he will take the route we might expect.

"Now let us get some rest, young one. My eyes feel like they are filled with sand."

CHAPTER FOURTEEN

The old woman died on the sixth day after Mad Wolf's trio left Rock Lake. Calling Loon didn't utter a sound, simply toppled off her pony to land with a dull thud beside the trail.

Ilona, tied to the pony's tail with both wrists bound before her, stepped to Calling Loon's side but was shoved away by Mad Wolf, who had kicked his own pony around in mid-stride and charged back to the scene.

"Huh. She is *nipewukun* . . . dead," he said in an indignant tone. "Too bad, but she was just an old woman, anyway. But you . . . you're young. A young slave is better than an old one. We go now. We have a long way ahead of us, and I am already hungry."

He dismounted only long enough to kick the old woman's body off the side of the trail, where it tumbled into the ravine below. With surprising agility for such an old man, Ilona thought, Mad Wolf leapt back on his pony, grabbed up the lead rope for the old woman's former mount, and led it away, dragging Ilona behind.

Ilona was truly sorry about Calling Loon's death. The old woman's skill with healing herbs and ointments had restored Ilona's strength to near normal, and she had come to like the old woman she helped with the camp work.

Food in Mad Wolf's camps was seldom of any quantity or quality, since the old recluse refused to take time from travel to do any serious hunting. But the efforts of the two women had resulted in a multitude of berries and nuts, and Calling Loon had managed to knock down some stupid spruce grouse at one point without even having to get off her horse.

She had also, at least to some extent, managed to ease Ilona's fears of her captor, although the girl still had a fanatical dread of the old man.

"He is a sick old man, and his mind is slipping," she had been told in muted tones the first day of her capture. "He might beat you a little bit sometimes, as he does me, and he never makes any sense when he talks, but I don't think he will ever *really* hurt you. Only do as you are told, and he will probably leave you alone most of the time.

"But don't try to argue with him or disagree with his crazy mumbling. It makes him more angry, and then he is dangerous."

Neither woman had dared to question Mad Wolf's objective in making Ilona walk behind Calling Loon's horse. It had begun on the morning of the fourth day, when he fastened a ten-foot rawhide rope to her bound hands and attached it to the pony's tail.

Now, with the old woman dead and the horse traveling relatively unburdened, Ilona had expected she would be allowed to ride, but for the moment at least, she dared not question her captor. Her moccasins were in tatters, and, although her feet were toughening, she still suffered from thorns, roots, and the occasional unavoidable stone.

But the old madman took little notice of her plight, except to halt the ponies and scream at her whenever she dared to fall, as he seemed to view her inadvertent and often painful tumbles.

"You are a clumsy slave. What is the matter with you? You must learn to walk much better than that before you can expect to ride a pony," he would cackle, repeating the phrase so often it became more a torture than the falls themselves.

But then, for no logical reason she could see, in anger sometimes accompanied by his willow switch, his story would change. "Get up and walk properly. It is far we must go, and I cannot always wait for you. *Kipimpa tan*—run! Or I'll have to beat you some more."

Often, it seemed the death of the old woman had served only to increase his madness. He often addressed Ilona as Calling Loon, most especially as she worked around the supper fire at night.

But each evening, before tucking himself into his vast pile of verminous robes, he made sure his young captive was securely fastened, often to his own wrist with the tether, and sometimes to a handy tree.

Takwakin, the autumn season, came to the mountains on the ninth night, coating trees and grass with a crisp mantle of frost. The sky was an ebony bowl, alive with twinkling stars. In the morning, there was a film of ice on the muskeg bogs and an uneasy hush over the land.

The old man awoke in a frenzy, and without even stopping to eat, began to load the ponies with their camp goods. Muttering incoherently all the while, he spoke to Ilona only enough to speed her actions in helping with the work.

She waited behind the old woman's pony, her tether dragging, not willing to risk another beating by antagonizing the old man, only to have him scream at her in a fury. "Get up on that horse, slave. We must travel far and fast today. Hurry! What a slow, clumsy slave you are."

Once she was astride, he grasped her tether and her pony's halter shank, clapped heels to his own mount, and cantered off down the trail. They rode all day, Mad Wolf refusing to halt for any sort of lunch, and, when evening approached, he sought a campsite more secluded than usual and cautioned Ilona to make only a small, smokeless fire.

She had noticed no indication they were being followed, but the old man's actions grew more and more erratic with each passing day, and soon she'd given up trying to make sense of it all. Tying her securely to a tree, he spent nearly an hour at dusk scouting—she assumed—along their back trail. And when he returned, his face black with anger, he hissed to her to keep quiet even though she'd made no sound.

Periodically throughout the night, curled tightly beneath the single skimpy robe he allowed her, she woke to find the old man prowling about the camp, muttering to himself and casting a wild eye at the swollen moon.

After such a night, she woke the next morning to the eerie, bugling call of a bull elk in a meadow below. Mad Wolf instantly delved into one of his many sacks of trinkets and charms, throwing things haphazardly in every direction until he located what he'd been seeking.

Rising, he threw back his head and began whistling back to the elk on a call made from a hollowed willow branch. Ilona had heard elk called before, but never in the fashion of Mad Wolf, who didn't seem to be trying to lure the beast within shooting range, but rather seemed to actually be conversing with the animal.

The piercing whistle softened to a series of guttural grunts, then rose again in blasts of frenzied bugling. After full dawn, the elk in the meadow ceased to answer, but Mad Wolf continued making strange little shrieks with the instrument even while Ilona was repacking the camp to his directions.

Throughout the day, her captor's madness seemed more and more vivid to the girl's apprehensive gaze. Sometimes chanting happily to himself, he would give way to a glowering silence, casting baleful looks at Ilona if she made the slightest noise.

That night, they camped early, well off the trail in a tiny hollow where a spring burbled from the side hill. Mad Wolf tied both horses securely where they could drink, then snubbed Ilona's tether to a tree and threw her sleeping robe at her with a command to stay silent.

"Do not try to escape, slave. I go to hunt the mighty *Wawaskesiw*—the bull elk. But I will leave my spirit brother here to watch you, and if you try to escape, or make any noise, he will beat you!"

The old man then gathered up his elk whistle and a short, powerful bow from his pack, smeared himself with a foul-smelling ointment from yet another package, and stalked off into the gloaming.

Moments later, Ilona heard the whistle sound far down the valley. Immediately, she began working on the rawhide bindings that held her wrists together. Without water, she couldn't stretch them enough to free herself, but by continuously working her wrists back and forth, she hoped to loosen them enough so she could get some purchase on the knot holding her tether to the tree.

Without warning, Mad Wolf stepped from the gathering shadows, a willow switch swinging in his hand. Savagely, he struck her across the head and shoulders, then methodically began to whip her swollen wrists.

"Did not I tell you my spirit brother would watch you, sneak? Now you will know that Mad Wolf does not lie. This time you will sit quietly, or he will call me back again, and if I have to return I will beat you some more."

He kicked her again for good measure, then strode back into the timber without a backward glance. Ilona spent the next two hours huddled shivering in the skimpy robe, cowering at every strange sound and fearful the madman would return to resume the beating.

Her wrists were shot with spasms of pain, both from the slowed circulation and the vicious whipping administered by

Mad Wolf. She could feel welts growing on her back and shoulders but felt sure she wasn't bleeding anywhere, at least. But, terrified or not, she most hated the fact that her injured wrists made her incapable of any new attempt to free herself.

Darkness had cloaked the camp when Mad Wolf returned, prancing along with a joint of elk meat over one shoulder and his body wrapped in a bloody, musky-smelling elk hide. Stirring up the coals, he transferred Ilona's tether to her neck, cut the bindings from her swollen wrists, and ordered her to enlarge the fire and cook a proper meal.

He began eating when the meat was only half cooked, gleefully smirking as the blood and grease ran down his face and chest.

"Am I not a great hunter?" he bragged to Ilona. "Who else among the Cree could slay the mighty *Wawaskesiw* so easily? With a single arrow, I did it. I called him to me, right out of the herd of his cows. He came out of the meadow and into the timber, and I slew him."

Leaping to his feet, the old man began to pantomime the details of his hunt, first sneaking along under the trees, then talking to the bull elk with the small willow whistle.

"I said to him, 'Come here, great one. I am only a small bull who wants to fight with you for your cows. Come and fight with me, or I will take all the females from you.'"

Ilona sat entranced by the vividness of his portrayal, seeing clearly in her mind the huge bull elk slashing through the willows in a red-eyed snorting fury. In the old man's gyrations, she could see the mighty antlers slashing right and left amongst the green willows, scattering bark and leaves as the herd master grunted and roared his defiance.

And then . . . the twanging bow, the mighty leap as an arrow burst through between the ribs to destroy the lung tissue; the few tottering steps as life fled in a spray of frothy blood; the final slow, moaning collapse of the dying monarch.

It was a pantomime in which Mad Wolf lost all semblance of humanity, becoming one with the bull elk he'd gone to slay, then—eerily—the smaller elk he described. She could feel the meadow grasses beneath his feet, smell the broken willow branches as the bull smashed his antlers against them in majestic fury.

The sounds of the elk bugling filled her ears, echoed in her brain. It was as if she were *there,* inside Mad Wolf but also invisible in the background, an observer eerily linked to the magic of the hunt, the slaying, the fall of the monarch.

Mad Wolf then returned to his gluttony, still wrapped in the bloody hide of his victim and mumbling nonsense through nearly toothless gums. Full dark had come and gone during his performance, and the moon had returned a brightness almost like daylight to the scene.

The rising moon brought with it a return of Mad Wolf's bestial insanity. Mumbling to himself in meaningless gibberish, he began to search among his collection of small packs and bundles.

Pieces of bone and horn and mummified bits of hide appeared in erratic order around the fire pit. The old man was half dancing, shuffling his feet to a tuneless cadence of grunts and moans.

Periodically, he cast a leering eye at Ilona, who had retreated to the limits of her tether, instinctively trying to make herself as inconspicuous as she could. She feared to look at him, lest it draw his attention further, but also feared not to watch, lest he attack her without warning.

Trembling with fear, she watched him strip off all his garments except the bloody elk hide. His own skin, she saw, was marked throughout with tattoos, ceremonial scarring, and shriveled pits left by the smallpox.

A withered tassel of manhood hung limp between his shrunken thighs, but even as she watched, he began to shake it in his hand as he danced with increased fervor around the fire-pit.

Head back, his mad, vacant eyes staring upward towards the moon, he pranced in an eerily rhythmic frenzy, tootling on his elk whistle and manipulating himself to greater proportions.

In the uncertain light he seemed to grow in stature, looming large against the background of the camp fire. Then he stopped, dead still. And Ilona's worst fears came to life as he strode toward her, *stalked* toward her, moving slowly and speaking slowly in a strangely gentle, crooning voice.

"This day I have slain the mighty *Wawaskesiw*. Now I have taken his spirit. I *am Wawaskesiw*. I have conquered. Now is the time for the breeding. Prepare yourself for my service. Kneel, that I may mount you. Kneel!"

The final word was no longer gentle, but a demand.

Paralyzed with mute horror, Ilona allowed herself to be dragged into the open and shoved to her knees before the dying fire. Her wrists still bound and her body in pain from his earlier whippings, she was helpless to resist. She shuddered as his rough hands ripped the hem of her tunic upward, and she felt the old man's spittle drool onto her neck as he positioned himself for the initial thrust.

Then the night was ruptured by a roar of rage, and her attacker was dragged from her and flung across the dying fire. Mad Wolf's grip on her hair pulled Ilona along with him for an instant before she managed to writhe away and avoid being dragged into the coals herself.

She recovered to see the old man, his bloodied elk skin flung aside, roll adroitly and come to his feet crouched like a trapped wolf, snarling, with slobber dripping down his chin and a bloodied knife rigid in his right hand.

Across the fire from him loomed a gigantic figure, arms outstretched as it rocked, growling in rage, eyes locked on the old man and his knife.

Savard? Her eyes closed in terror as the combatants lurched at each other. Bent over double, Ilona scrambled back to the limits of her tether, trying to keep as far from the battle as she could get, afraid to watch, afraid not to watch.

Afraid.

CHAPTER FIFTEEN

Garth Cameron circled the fire cautiously, but clumsily, and cursed himself for his own stupidity. He had sorely underestimated his opponent who had shouted, "Mad Wolf has taken the spirit of *Wawaskesiw!*"

When he'd flung the old man across the fire, he had expected the wizened madman to be out of the fight almost immediately.

Crazy, perhaps, and certainly old, but the man who called himself Mad Wolf had forgotten more about knife fighting than Garth would learn for years to come. The old man had twisted in mid-air, landed almost on his feet, and grasped a knife from beside the flames even as he came upright.

Now Garth panted as he felt his strength already leaving him. The left sleeve and the front of his elk-skin shirt were black with blood, and he could feel his vision blurring, his eyes glazing over with anger and shock.

Mostly anger, which was what kept him alert as he and Mad Wolf circled the fire, each with a knife in one hand, each making little feinting movements but not quite coming to grips.

In the first encounter, to Garth's surprise, the old man had leapt the fire, slashed right and left in a blur of motion, then leapt back again, leaving Garth with a useless left arm and a shallow but painful cut across his lower chest.

Only his youthful reflexes had kept him from losing the fight with that first engagement, he knew. Resolved not to die foolishly, he ceased being overconfident and fell into a deadly, serious calm. Not even Ilona's gasp when she looked up and recognized him could distract his attention from the fight.

It seemed it would go on forever, this cautious circling, turning, circling in the other direction, but then Mad Wolf erupted with a defiant scream and leapt forward in a series of flashing thrusts. Sparks flew as Garth countered with his own knife and then, awkwardly, put all his strength into a right-handed shove that drove the old man back.

Pain and loss of blood were beginning to tell on Garth, and the knowledge drew Mad Wolf into a flurry of attacks. Always, Garth managed to counter, but each effort cost him in strength, and he couldn't do much more than defend himself.

Realizing he had to end the fight soon or succumb to his growing weariness, he eased closer and closer to the fire, deliberately feigning weakness. Then, in a last-gasp spurt of energy, he kicked into the flames, throwing a cloud of ashes and smoldering coals at his naked opponent.

Recoiling from the hot coals, Mad Wolf was thrown slightly off balance. Before he could recover, Garth planted a well-aimed kick to the old man's groin.

Clutching at himself in agony, Mad Wolf staggered away, seeking room to maneuver. It brought him within reach of Ilona's position, and she thrust out with both feet against the small of his back, throwing him forward almost into the fire and directly into the arc of Garth's flashing knife. The weapon flashed downward, then up in a bloody curve, and the old man crumpled to the earth.

Wiping the bloodied knife blade on his leggings, Garth turned with a sickly smile toward Ilona, took three wavering steps, then collapsed at her feet.

Sobbing with relief and the terror that he might have been killed, she snatched up the knife, quickly rid herself of the tether and manacles, then knelt to assess the damage to her savior.

Unable to roll him closer to the fire without doing more damage, she slashed off his shirt and began cleansing and binding his wounds. Once again she sobbed with relief when she discovered the chest wound was relatively minor. But the other one . . .

Nonetheless, she was inordinately pleased at being able to deal with Garth's wounds while he was unconscious, leaving her free to consider how she would eventually manage dealing with the man himself.

Ilona knew Garth's reputation, if only from hearsay. The tale of his escape from the Blackfoot had swooped like a fog through the post at Rocky Mountain House and the adjacent free traders' camp and had been embellished with every telling. In her heart she knew he had been captured while involved in a brief dalliance with the chief's young wife, but by the time the story got around, Garth had been credited with seducing every maiden in the entire Blackfoot camp.

Not hard to understand how such a thing might happen—she didn't deny his attractiveness, and of course his position in the company of David Thompson showed he was highly thought of.

And my papa likes him . . . I know that. He never believed the nonsense Savard tried to spread after I was shot. All those lies, but even I did not know what was truth, at first. And he is tres *brave, is he not?*

She wallowed in the memory of Garth, his fiery hair and beard glowing like flame from the campfire and moonlight during the fight. Not difficult to understand how naïve young Indian girls would nickname him "Sun Buffalo," for his virile strength and the color of his hair.

He was a handsome specimen—no doubt of that. The problem now was to ensure he didn't die from the old man's knife, not whether she could have any place in the life she now sought to save.

"And I am a fool to be thinking about such things," she said aloud to herself. "He will return to the east when his time comes, and I am Peigan. My place is here with my father and our people. My father, he is the leader of the free trappers, and even without that we could return to live with my mother's people on the buffalo plains, where I belong. I have seen enough of how the women of my people are left behind by the traders and voyageurs, left with Métis children and memories. It is not enough."

Days later, Garth rested lazily against a convenient log, his left arm firmly bound in clean bandages and the sun warm against his bare chest. With growing admiration, he watched the slim figure of Ilona as she busied herself with the camp chores. The gash across his lower chest was unbandaged but coated with a smelly mixture of grease and spruce gum the girl had gently applied.

He found it difficult to ignore the allure of Ilona's presence. She moved about the camp with quiet efficiency, dealt with his wounds in the same manner, but was difficult to figure out some of the time. Most of the time. She was, in turns, efficient, direct, and open . . . then quiet, reserved, almost shy, it seemed.

He found her breathtakingly beautiful, but there was far more to it than that, and he couldn't help but wonder if she, too, had feelings embroiled in the strangeness of their situation.

For three days, he'd rested, Ilona steadfastly refusing his suggestions that they had to move south—and soon—in a bid to find René.

"The old one can wait," she'd said. "The cut on your chest must heal a bit before you can ride safely, and I am afraid for your left arm. That cut was very deep, and, without proper care, you could lose the use of the arm. We stay here."

Her only concession had been to let him hold and steady a

pony while she lashed Mad Wolf's body behind it on what had been her tether. Then she'd managed to drag the body a half-mile down the trail to where she could place it under a steep, overhanging cut bank. It was easy enough then to use a broken spruce snag to pry the rim loose and cover the corpse with clay and loose rock.

"*Muchi napew*—an evil man, that one," she had said when it was done. "At least now he will not draw more trouble to the camp. Now let us go away from here. It makes my stomach sick even to be near him."

"He was a tough old man," Garth replied, "and I see now how much I underestimated him. Careless . . . and it damned near got me killed. Not a good recommendation if I'm supposed to protect you."

"Protect me? Is that why you're here—to protect me?"

Garth was nettled by the patent incredulity in her voice but chose—wisely, he thought—to ignore it. "It's what we've been trying to do ever since that bastard Savard kidnapped you back at Rocky Mountain House, although I'm not surprised you didn't notice. We haven't been doing the job very well."

It shamed him to make the admission, but the truth was self-evident, and he had no doubts about this woman's ability to sort truth from nonsense. Everything about her was impressive, from her superb horsemanship to her knowledge of how to live off the country.

From his days and days of tracking her, following where she had suffered through the icy waters and brambles and muskegs and sand flies and blackflies, he reckoned this girl named Climbing Woman was tougher than he, and perhaps smarter than René, in the bargain.

Garth was most impressed with the girl's neat, efficient attitude around their camp. Fully recovered from her own ordeal with Mad Wolf, she seemed . . . not shy, exactly, but definitely reserved.

In dressing his wounds, she was crisply efficient, yet seemed to avoid touching him except when absolutely necessary. She seldom looked at Garth directly, but always with downcast eyes. Unless directly spoken to, she seldom spoke, and then only in murmurs. Garth found this reserve somewhat disconcerting, but also attractive. She was decidedly a different temperament from the other Indian women he'd known since coming west.

Garth, knowing they had a long ride ahead back to Rocky Mountain House and that they might be forced by the weather into wintering together somewhere en route, didn't press himself upon Ilona. She would not respond well, he thought, to his normally ebullient nature, and he found himself unsure exactly how to approach her.

There was no doubt in his own mind that he had begun to feel . . . different about this native woman than he ever had about Indian girls in the past, but it wasn't a difference he could quite explain to himself; and certainly nothing he could begin to discuss with his beautiful, enigmatic companion.

The last of Mad Wolf's elk meat was gone by the fifth day, and, with Garth's wounds healing cleanly, if slowly, he announced they would break camp the next day at dawn. Ilona made no reply, except for the briefest of nods, but began collecting the various necessities and loads for the three ponies. She had brought Garth's mount in on the morning after he'd found Mad Wolf's camp.

Garth had little idea about where they might find old René, especially since he knew they'd have to be careful and consider any strangers to be enemies. Savard was still . . . somewhere . . . and any of the Cree were as likely to be feared as helpful. Not for the first time, he regretted not having René's skills and fluency with the various native languages. If they did meet any

Indians before they found his friend and mentor, he'd be dependent on Ilona to communicate, which might be a problem.

But he expected René would keep close to the trails along Sheep Creek, if he could, and would certainly attempt to leave him some signs that only he would be able to interpret. The ponies were well rested and eager to move, so they made good time.

Finding René was easier than expected. Too easy, in fact. They were halfway across the creek two mornings later when the old voyageur came thundering down a ridge on the other side, with three screaming Cree a quarter-mile behind.

René's arms were flapping madly as he urged his pony along. With his own small body bouncing high on the horse's withers, he looked almost laughable. But there was no time to laugh, and it was not a laughing matter.

Thrusting the reins into Ilona's waiting hand, Garth dropped from his pony in mid-stream, calling to René and checking his rifle priming at the same time.

"Ho! Little monkey . . . over here!"

It was awkward for Garth to steady the heavy rifle. His left arm in its sling made the operation difficult, and he was clumsy finding his target. But his first shot dropped the leading Cree pony in a flurried tangle of horse and rider.

René, by this time, had his own weapon in action. He killed one Cree with his first shot and downed a horse with the second before Garth could clumsily reload his own rifle. The third rider turned away, grabbing up the uninjured first rider as he did so. They were out of range before Garth was ready to shoot again.

"*Mon Dieu*," René cried with a laugh. "Never have I been so glad to see a friendly face. Come now, let us depart this place before those Indian they decide to fight some more. The middle of a river is no place for a shooting war, anyway."

Leaping on his pony, he led them on a hectic ride over half a dozen ridges before pulling up in a sheltered glade and dismounting so he could rush over to greet Garth.

"You have been fighting without me," he said in accusatory tones as he inspected Garth's wounds. "So, we will make camp here. There is plenty of feed for the horses, and I think our Indian friends they will not want to walk so far with only their one horse.

"So now, my friend, I think you have some story to tell old René. I see you have found your elusive little pigeon. Perhaps little Climbing Woman she will cook us some fine deer steak I have in my saddlebags, and you will tell me all of your adventure . . . *non*?"

They spent the evening recounting their various adventures, Ilona contributing little at first, but then, under René's humorous persuasion, vividly pantomiming for him her experiences with the old madman.

She devoted time to re-enact—as old Mad Wolf had done— the crazy old man's depiction of his stalking and slaying of *Wawaskesiw*, the bull elk, and both men sat mesmerized by the clarity and vividness of her performance. They sat entranced as she took, by turns, the parts of Mad Wolf, the dominant bull elk and the fake interloper. Then she switched scenarios and revealed—from her own point of view—how the hunt and what followed had stimulated the old madman into the situation Garth had thankfully interrupted. Afterward, she hung her head for a moment in reflection, then threw her gaze to the stars and flashed a thankful smile to her savior.

"It is over now. I will not speak of it again," she said.

By moonrise, the wrinkled old voyageur and the slender maiden were joking and laughing together in her own language while Garth hovered silently around the edges. He could understand only the occasional word of René's conversation with Ilona and seemed unsure as to why Ilona would be so friendly with René but so shy with him. Garth's experiences with native girls had all been of the fleeting, direct, usually sexual nature. He had never been exposed to Ilona's more sophisticated, indirect flirtation.

René, of course, had spent half his life in Indian camps, and he'd been the target of such antics many times. He was taking a huge delight in the boy's suffering and discomfort. At one point, indeed, he considered clueing Garth to the game but then thought better of it.

"Huh. Serves the young fool right," he muttered. "René, he's going to let the little Climbing Woman play her games. She likes the boy, but she will make him chase her until she is ready to catch him, for sure . . . and only if she really wants to."

Garth's arm wound had reopened during the day's hard riding, so in the morning, René elected to scout the surrounding region while the younger man rested. René only laughed at Garth's protests, waving to Ilona and calling back over his shoulder as he rode off, "Do not be ashamed of your weakness, young one. When I was your age I would have jumped at the chance to stay alone in camp with such a lovely maiden." And then—in Ilona's language: "Treat him well, Climbing Woman. He is big and strong and only a little bit stupid. If you try hard enough, maybe you can teach him Peigan or Cree so he won't have to sulk around the fire at night."

Ilona, while Peigan Blackfoot in her heritage, was fluent in both languages, not least because her father was a free trapper, and Cree was the dominant language of trade along the North Saskatchewan and the other rivers that flowed east from the mountains.

She laughed at René's jest, but had her own ideas about dealing with young Garth Cameron. Ilona had been raised to value herself highly in the overall scheme of things . . . not a snob, by any means, but she was the daughter of an important man, and it often showed in her poise and dignity.

René rode away, chuckling merrily to himself, and deliberately spent the entire day and half the evening prowling north and west around the camp, looking for signs of trouble—Savard, especially, but also signs of hostile Indians and the trails they might be using regularly. He returned just at dusk with an expression of resigned displeasure on his wrinkled face.

"The situation, it is not a good one," he said once he'd tended to his pony and was slouched against a handy tree with a chunk of venison warm in his hands. "Sleeping Elk's men are all stirred up and prowling like hungry wolves, especially along the trails to the south. I think if we want to stay safe we must look to the north and face the fact that winter is coming and soon. We will have to face it somewhere, because it is too far now and too late in the season to make it back to Rocky Mountain House, even on the best of trails, and they are closed to us.

"I have heard that somewhere on a river to the north of us are big flats where always some Cree and Iroquois winter," René continued, "but not Sleeping Elk's people, I don't think, so it should be safe enough for us.

"The heavy snows will be here in two weeks, and we cannot winter here. We must be somewhere that is safe, and somewhere we can be sure of feed for the horses and have plenty of firewood and game to be hunted.

"So we go north, eh? The Iroquois they will not fight with us or any other white men, but if they are there on the *Kakwa* . . . the Porcupine River . . . I am sure they would welcome us and give us company and help to get through the winter. What say you?"

Ilona demurred from comment. Garth, with no reasonable alternative in mind, said he'd be pleased to follow René's lead and steadfast logic, so the next day they set out on the trails to the north, following René's instincts along a skein of winding, twisting, moose and caribou trails through the dark forests, crossing streams, skirting muskeg bogs and—always—alert to danger from man or beast at every turn of the trails to the north, toward the Kakwa River and the safe wintering grounds it might offer them.

A week later they rode cautiously down the long, slow descent into the valley of the Kakwa River to find wild hay belly deep on the ponies in the rich alluvial soil and moose, deer, and even an occasional forest buffalo scattered before them like cattle in a pasture.

A cluster of cabins huddled under the lee of a spruce bluff on the meadow's edge, and a dozen brown faces appeared in doorways as the three rode cautiously forward.

"Iroquois, as I said we'd find," murmured René. "One or two Cree, also, I'm thinking. But they look friendly enough, so let me speak with them and see how rough this winter she'll be. It may be that they will welcome us as extra hunters, which are always welcome in a camp with many mouths to feed."

A tall, proud-looking man strode forward as René approached the cabins. René dismounted, and the two shook hands, white man fashion, before squatting cross-legged on the grass to begin a lengthy, slow conversation.

About half an hour passed, with Garth becoming increasingly wary and nervous, before his old friend clambered on his pony and returned to them, smiling broadly.

"Aaah . . . it will be a good winter, I'm thinking. These are the people of Henri Wanyandie, and they are surely peaceable. Iroquois, as I thought. The headman he has invited us to spend the winter with them, and he is glad to see us because he has few young men to hunt, and his medicine man says the winter will be a long, cold one, with many storms. The river, and these meadows here, they are named for *le Kakwa,* the porcupine, because there are many of them in the area. Sometimes that is a good thing, because the porcupine is one animal that a man can hunt without any weapon but a stick, if need be, but a camp like this needs real meat, and a lot of it, to get through a long, cold winter."

Cheerfully, they kicked their horses forward, then stopped dead in their tracks as the door of the cabin next to the chief's opened and out stepped Savard, grinning wolfishly and openly ogling Ilona.

Garth was for leaving immediately, and he didn't much care in which direction they went. Ilona said nothing, but her caution of Savard needed no words. René, after a second conversation with Wanyandie, was adamant in his conviction that they should stay in the Iroquois encampment . . . and indeed that they had little genuine choice.

"Consider this," he said. "No matter where we go now, Savard can follow if he chooses. Here, he cannot really do much without risking his own hide. I have talked to the chief, and he knows of Savard and does not really want him here, but these are a peaceable people and they will not force him—or us—out of their camp. But also they will not allow trouble in the camp . . . not from anyone. Wanyandie assures me of that, and he is an honorable man. I am sure that if Savard starts any trouble, they will send him away.

"Now the same goes for us. Myself, I think we're safer here. Ilona can move in with one of the families where there is a daughter of somewhat her own age. She cannot stay with us. The Iroquois have strict rules about such things."

"I still don't like it," Garth growled and looked to Ilona for support. But she would neither meet his eyes nor answer his demand for support. As their prospective hosts moved out of the cabins and came to greet them, it was clear the camp was composed of tight family groups, with several young women who appeared to be Ilona's age.

"We can guard her easily enough," René suggested. "There are two of us, and if there is always one of us here to keep an eye on Savard, it should be no problem. Once we are wintered in, things should remain peaceful enough, but you have my word that at the first sign of trouble I will shoot him like the dog that he is, and I know you, too, will have the same caution."

He paused, then added, "Of course they might throw us out of their camp if we kill Savard, but at least we won't have to watch our back trail as we go."

Garth remained apprehensive. Savard, he knew, was cunning as a wolf and was almost certain to give them some sort of problems during the confinement of a long winter. To make things worse, even in the short time since their arrival, he'd noticed several of the younger Iroquois men making eyes at Ilona.

"Dammit, René, I don't like the setup at all," he said. "You know how cunning and devious that half-breed bastard can be. Look at the things he's already done! I vote we shoot him now and take our chances. The worst that might happen is we'd have to winter somewhere else, and this can't be the only decent wintering ground in the area."

Henri Wanyandie directed them to a vacant cabin on the edge of the camp and left the three of them to unload the ponies, but only moments later he was back, and, when they replied to his knock at the door, he entered, followed by a clearly disgruntled Savard.

Nodding to Garth and René, the chief began a long, slow oratory, mingling Cree and Iroquois—both unintelligible to Garth. Nonetheless, Wanyandie managed to get his message across. Pointing first to Savard and then to Ilona, he cut his hand across his throat in a chopping motion that needed no words, although René couldn't resist translating the obvious to Garth.

"He tells Savard that he must not so much as look at your little Climbing Woman in the wrong way, or he will have his throat cut without hesitation," René said. "He says there will be peace here in the camp, or there will be much bloodshed, and Savard's will be first."

Turning, the chief ordered Savard out of the cabin in tones that brooked no argument; then he turned to Ilona and began a lengthy discussion in broken Cree. Ilona listened without interruption, then nodded meekly and stooped to gather her blankets and gear and followed him out the door without so much as a farewell to Garth and René.

Garth, flushed with anger at being so ignored, had half risen from his couch of robes when René almost casually shoved him back down. When the door had closed, René rounded on Garth with obvious and genuine anger of his own.

"Now listen to me, young Garth . . . and listen well! Some day you are going to get us both killed, you. *Sacré!* I do wish you would hurry up and learn Cree. The old chief he says that your little Climbing Woman she will spend the winter in his lodge. He has no sons, but there are two daughters about her own age to keep her company. This is an honor for her, do you not see this?"

He shook his head as if to clear away his anger, then continued, leaning down over Garth and staring him in the eyes as he hissed out the details of what had transpired. "He offers her his protection, and she has taken it. A smart girl, that one. If Savard should bother the girl, the chief's daughters will know immediately, and every hand in this camp will be against him. Savard has been here only a week, I think, and already he is not well thought of. There is a chance they will send him away just because of that; we both know how volatile his temper is and how quick he is to start fights. With any luck he will get himself run out of this camp without us being involved at all. The situation is as ideal as it can be, for us."

He told the young man to rest while he conferred further with the Iroquois chieftain, but halfway out the door he turned abruptly and ducked back inside. *"Mon Dieu!* Why can nothing ever go right? Look out there, young Garth, and see our next big problem."

Garth peeked through the partly opened door and saw Sleeping Elk, war bonnet waving in the breeze, staring angrily down at Henri Wanyandie from the back of a tall, piebald pony. Across the meadow, running their ponies back and forth like children and shouting derisively, were half a dozen Sunchild Cree warriors.

René, peering under Garth's arm, struggled to follow the complicated sign language being used between the two chieftains and translated as the conversation went on.

"Sleeping Elk, he says he does not want war with these people. That is something, at any rate," René explained. "But he wants . . . Savard! That is a surprise, and it would be good except that he also wants us, my friend.

"Wanyandie says that we are all guests in his camp and he will not give us up. He says if Sleeping Elk wants to make a fight of it, then a fight he can have. There are seventeen armed men, he says, waiting in the cabins—all armed and ready to start shooting if necessary. He is lying, of course, but he is doing it well. I think Sleeping Elk is fooled.

"Damn it! Wanyandie would like to give them Savard, from the sound of it, but it would be against his honor to do so, and Sleeping Elk knows that, too. He is backing down."

The Cree turned and headed back up the ridge, some of the younger men shouting taunts back over their shoulders, but obviously the situation had been defused, and, with both chieftains in accord, nobody else would push the issue any further.

Wanyandie, head bowed in troubled thought, strolled over to their cabin once the Cree were out of sight and began a long discourse with René. The old voyageur motioned to Garth, who took the cue and left his elders alone while he made a leisurely examination of the Iroquois encampment.

Passing near the chief's cabin, he heard a partially stifled giggle and turned to see Ilona with two tall, attractive young women about her own age as they retreated around the corner. Curious, he followed and found himself "it" in an impromptu game of tag with three beautiful native girls. Giggling shrilly, they scampered back and forth around the structure, affording the young man only brief glimpses of flashing black eyes and trim ankles.

Then, as suddenly as they had appeared, they were gone. And in their place a stern-faced old squaw whose derisive cackle left the young Cameron blushing to the roots of his copper-colored hair. He hadn't understood a word, but the old woman's contempt needed no specifics.

René's laughter, when Garth returned to their cabin and voiced his confusion, was no balm to his shattered feelings.

"Ha ha . . . three beauties! What a winter you are going to have, my young friend. Have you made a choice yet, or will you wait until the time of the *suskin yootin,* the snow-eating Chinook winds? You'd best be cautious, young one. Remember the old saying about a bird in the hand. Still . . . maybe there will be some mixed-blood babies in the camp next winter if Ilona should fall for one of these tall Iroquois braves, and you can tie down one of the chief's daughters, *non?*"

The old man chuckled at his friend's discomfort and seemed to relish the opportunities to tease him. "If you are not too

greedy, there might even be one small Iroquois left over for old
René, to warm his feet on the cold winter nights, and at least
maybe by spring you would have learned one Indian language,
although Cree would be of more use to you than Iroquois. Only
a few of these people came west with the first voyageurs, and
there are fewer yet who decided to stay."

He explained how the Iroquois had been among the first natives to take up trading with the early French traders along the
Great Lakes, but he soon tired of playing teacher.

"What do you say to some supper, eh? If you are going to
take on all three of these lovely young women you'd best do so
on a full belly. Come. The chief has invited us to eat this night
in his cabin, and to refuse would be bad manners. Maybe you
will see more of your three girlfriends, although it is doubtful.
The Iroquois women usually don't eat with their men. But the
food should be worth our time. They killed a young dry buffalo
cow only yesterday.

"Ah," he sighed. "Some fat hump meat would do this old
man's heart good."

CHAPTER SIXTEEN

The Iroquois chief was uncannily correct in his assessment of the season to come. The winter could be summarized in a single word: cold.

Garth Cameron found the cold bearable, even while doing his share of guarding the pony herd, but the boredom! He missed the bustle of Rocky Mountain House and similar posts, where even in winter there was sufficient work required to keep even a young man's mind and muscles busy.

But for him, the worst aspects of wintering on the Kakwa involved the constant teasing and flirting and tormenting he had to endure from Ilona and her two new friends. The three, together, kept him in a constant torment of love and lust and uncertainty.

Despite the language barrier, Ilona got on well with her new friends, Elise and Monique, the chief's daughters. All three spoke considerable French—another language in which Garth was hopelessly deficient—and spent a good deal of time teaching each other Peigan Blackfoot, Cree, and Iroquois.

René, finding the chief spoke considerable French, spent long hours in conversation with him, learning about the region, the terrain, and the river systems, while attempting to improve his knowledge of the Iroquois customs and language. Wanyandie and his people had come west with the first trading expedition along the North Saskatchewan River to the Rockies, René told Garth. They liked the country, and stayed . . . gradually moving north to avoid conflict with the Blackfoot and Cree who lived closer to the prairie buffalo grounds.

Garth also attempted to learn Iroquois, but by December he virtually gave it up, convinced he could never be a linguist and becoming increasingly despondent as a result.

"You are going about it the wrong way, my young friend," counseled René. "What you must do is select one of these three lovely, petite maidens and persuade her to teach you her language and the ways of her people. How do you think old René, he is learning all the languages along the river systems from Montreal to these mountains?"

"Easier said than done; I can't hardly understand the Iroquois language at all." Garth was still confused as a result of yet another incident in which he'd been the butt of jokes by the three native women. He knew that René could have told him what the jokes meant, but his friend seemed to be enjoying the games too, if only as an observer.

"Besides," Garth continued. "How can anyone make a selection when the girls are never alone?"

In the generally confused state in which he was kept by the three young women, he had yet to realize that he was actually the target of some fierce competition.

Initially recognizing Ilona's prior claim, the Iroquois girls had come to regard Ilona's shyness with Garth as a lack of interest, and now the competition was heating up. René knew this, of course, but was loath to make things easier for Garth. He, himself, had survived such antics in his younger years along the rivers and considered it all part of his young friend's education.

What Garth interpreted as a sort of plot against him René knew to be only a refusal by any of the girls to give the others the slightest advantage. They watched each other whenever the red-haired young giant was anywhere near and spent their spare time hatching plots and counterplots against each other.

Meanwhile, Savard was proving to be another huge surprise of the otherwise boring winter. Apparently taking the chief's warning to heart, he'd devoted his time to running an extensive trap line and was seldom in the small settlement at all, except when he came by to drop off a welcome hindquarter of moose or venison or mountain caribou, then guide a party of young men out to claim the rest of the meat.

Garth and René also hunted, but with somewhat less success, mostly because Savard was trapping well beyond the usual areas of native activity, so the game he sought and bagged was undisturbed and easy to hunt.

Garth did, however, run his own trap line in a different direction from Savard's claim and by Christmas had amassed not only several beaver, but three exceptionally fine wolf pelts. Two of them were blacks, but the third, even larger, was an unusual creamy, almost golden color.

He had convinced the old woman who sometimes cooked for him and René to tan the furs and at René's suggestion was planning to give them to the three young women as Christmas presents.

His major difficulty was in deciding who should get the golden hide, obviously the rarer of the three. Garth still fancied himself in love with Ilona but had to admit he found the brazen charms of Monique, the eldest of the chief's daughters, difficult to resist.

"Bah," said René, who was by now getting disgusted with having to listen to Garth expound upon the various charms of the girls. "You young ones have no sense. First, we chase halfway across the mountains to rescue the little Climbing Woman, Ilona, and you can think of nothing else. Now, you see a pair of round Iroquois buttocks and all you can think of is that thing between your thighs.

"Enough! You can have one of them or try to run off with them all, like you are some sort of bull elk, but speak no more to René about these three girls. Tomorrow, I go to live with the widow, Red Willow. She has been without a man for two seasons, and she is old enough to know what she wants, without all this playing of games."

René, without Garth noticing, had already collected his few personal belongings, and, from the look on the old woodsman's face, it was clear to Garth that René was serious about spending the rest of the winter away from Garth and his chattering, giggling, provocative tormentors.

"You, my horny young friend, you can stay here and play house with all three of your pretty vixens. I remind you that the chief might object mightily if you stretch the bounds of his hospitality too far, so be careful. These are good people, here . . . people with standards they expect to have respected. *Certainement*, accidents . . . happen, but it is expected a visitor should do the right thing. Only remember that when spring comes, old René is riding south, and we only have four horses. One of them is for the packing, and one is for me. Unless you want to walk all the way back to Rocky Mountain House, you'd best make up your mind by then, because you cannot take all three of the lovely young women with us."

With that, René gathered his duffle and stomped out the door.

Garth's Christmas present problem was staved off when one of the Iroquois boys rushed into the settlement one morning to report a mountain lion had raided the pony herd. Before his very eyes, the panicked boy swore, a cougar as large as a full-grown horse had charged into the herd, picked up a yearling colt, and carried it off.

Surely, someone said, it must be the same cougar that had

decimated the herd two winters before and killed two men when they cornered it on a rock ledge later in the winter.

From the Indians' viewpoint, the issue was resolved. They would try to guard the pony herd better, but nobody would dare to seek out and try to kill a man-killing cougar. It would be suicide, they said. The cat was obviously an evil spirit sent to plague them.

And from that point the conversation detoured into ponderings about who and why and for what reasons the evil spirit had come. Not surprisingly, Savard's name came up, but so did those of René and Garth. In the face of superstition, strangers became as suspect as any other ill omen.

René put up with it for a few minutes, then tried to bring some sanity to it all.

"A full-grown cougar will take a horse every four days if there is no other game," he said. "At least once a week, anyway. And we know there is little other game anywhere close to this settlement. Think upon this: at that rate, by spring there will not be a horse in the valley. Clearly, we must kill the beast."

But the superstitious elements of the problem erupted yet again, and René stomped off in disgust, following Garth back to the cabin where the young man now lived with two unmarried Iroquois men . . . not that it served to help his language skills all that much.

"These superstitious Iroquois will not hunt the cougar," he raged. "Not even if it costs them every horse they own. But René, he is not walking back to Rocky Mountain House if he can help it."

The decision was followed by a knock on the cabin door, and in strode Savard, not waiting for any invitation, followed by Chief Henri Wanyandie.

"Peace," Savard growled. "This problem of the *misi pisiw*—the cougar—is more important than our little disagreement."

Savard, like René, was concerned for the horses and even more so by the superstitious attitude of their hosts. It was vital, he said, that they put aside their enmity and join forces to get rid of the mountain lion now, before it destroyed any more horses.

"This one, he and I together will hunt the cat," Savard said, pointing to Garth. "But first we shall swear before the chief to guard each other's life with our own, and one shall not return without the other."

Garth, reluctantly, swore the oath, but under his breath he took another . . . to guard his own back against treachery from Savard. Then the two men gathered their gear and set out to track the cat. René, it was determined, should stay in the settlement, where his superior shooting skills might be needed if the cat returned to attack the horse herd, which had been brought in close to the cabins.

Three days later Garth and Savard had followed the cat in a great circle to the east and then north again, when they came upon the scene where the cougar had killed a young mule deer, then cached the remains high in a convenient tree.

"That is one pony saved, for the moment. He will return to this kill, I think," Savard said. "We must ambush the creature, but be careful that *misi pisiw* does not ambush us!"

They took up positions on opposite sides of the spot, each of them well hidden but less than a hundred yards from the carcass. The easiest, most logical approach to the tree, they left open. In the oncoming darkness, Garth could see the cache in the tree crotch, and beyond it the bulk of Savard, huddled beneath the low spreading branches of a scrub pine.

Garth was squatting against a tree trunk, huddled warmly in his blanket and struggling to stay awake and alert, when he saw flame leap from the muzzle of Savard's rifle and heard the whistle of the ball as it hissed past his ear.

"Damn! I missed the bastard," swore the black bearded woodsman. "Why did you not shoot? He jumped practically right over your head."

But Garth, sputtering with rage, trained his own rifle on Savard.

"You son-of-a-bitch! You were trying to hit me, not the cat. And don't try to lie your way out of it, because we both know there was no cougar here this night."

"*Mais non.* You do me a wrong, young one. Here, Savard will light the torch, and you can see for yourself that the beast truly was here. And if I lie, you have light then to shoot me, *non?*"

Without even waiting for a reply, the big man laid aside his rifle and struck flame to a pitch-soaked torch. Then he stomped through the snow toward Garth, not bothering to even look at him, but instead searching the snow-covered ground between them.

And there, unmistakable in the torchlight, were the tracks of the cougar, exactly as the burly woods boss had claimed. Even Garth could see by the spoor that the cat had approached the cache, then somehow been spooked—perhaps by Savard ready-ing for his shot—and leaped right over Garth in a bid for escape.

Garth tried to form an apology, but it soured in his mouth even as Savard ignored it.

"See? Savard does not lie. Did we not swear a truce, you and I? Surely you do not think Louis Savard would break his word?"

But the expression in the big man's dark eyes put doubt on the remark, and Garth knew that, if anything, their alliance was at even greater risk now. It was a sobering thought.

Nearly a week went by before they caught up to the cat again, and in that time the two woodsmen realized they had essentially circled the Kakwa settlement and were back near where the first kill had occurred. The animal clearly had been heading for the usual pony pasture when it happened on an old, lame caribou and chose the easier prey instead. The blood was still soft on the snow when the men took up the track, plodding laboriously on their snowshoes toward the crest of the ridge.

"This time we will get him for sure," Savard said, frost silvering his breath and bristly black beard. "I'm pretty sure he'll go back to where we almost treed him before. These big cats usually have a special place to den up for the winter, someplace high up."

They trudged all day without spotting the cat, then camped in a sheltering spruce thicket as fresh snow began to sift down. Savard remained convinced the cat would continue his usual routine. Garth was less certain but also had to admit he was far less experienced.

His thoughts were occupied with the coming of Christmas, only three days away. Now, squatting beside their small fire, he was lost in thought when Savard's words registered with him.

". . . only three days from now. Have you got the presents for all your girlfriends? Which one is your favorite, I wonder. The little Climbing Woman, or the long-legged Iroquois, Monique? Ah, that one could keep a man warm through a long winter. Such legs! In Cree, she would be named *Misi moohka hasiw,* the heron. I tell you, if she ever wraps those long legs around you, you will follow that Iroquois woman until you die . . . and that should not take too long. She'd probably squeeze the life out of you on your first night with her, eh?"

Not being disposed to discuss his love life with the huge half-breed, least of all in the crude terms Savard seemed to favor, Garth didn't bother to reply, but this didn't cut off the flow of obscene speculation from his unwelcome companion, who took huge delight in baiting Garth.

"That young Climbing Woman, she has a good body, too. I

noticed that when I pulled her out of the Nordegg River last spring. A little small in the breasts, perhaps, but enough to give you a grip when you ride her, eh? We could ask the brothers Cardinal. Both of them had their pleasure, too, with her before I killed them. You didn't know that, Cameron? You don't think Savard he would waste all this time chasing an untried mare."

The big man chuckled, peering slyly at Garth before he continued.

"Ah . . . that was a trip we had back from the Nordegg crossing. The first time, of course, she was a little groggy from that misplaced bullet, but the second time, and the third . . . *Mon Dieu!* That one she could spend half her life on her back and still beg for more. I tell you, if I'd had her for another week, she'd have followed Louis Savard forever, begging—"

With a strangled roar, Garth lunged from his blanket, unable to listen anymore despite a half-certain knowledge he was being played. Knife in hand and all caution thrown to the winds, he came upright to find himself staring down the muzzle of Savard's long rifle.

"Now, you will please to sit back down and mind your manners. Remember, please, the oath that you swore, that we *both* swore. You shall guard my back, and I shall in turn guard yours, but I took no oath of silence.

"If you do not like what I have to say, then do not listen. But do not come waving that little knife at me anymore or I shall have to take it from you and break a finger or two, so don't become a blasphemer. It is late, now. Go to sleep, young Cameron, and dream nice things about your little girlfriend and how she liked Savard, hey?"

Garth struggled awake after a nearly sleepless night, half convinced he should ignore the vow and kill Savard where he lay, but the burly woods boss was up before him, rifle in hand

and the tea pail in the other. He said nothing, but his alertness was sufficient to keep Garth cautious as they prepared a quick breakfast and then hit the trail.

At noon, they cut the cougar's tracks again, so fresh there were granules of snow still filtering into the pad marks. They were high on the ridge by this time, and the track led straight to a bare, rocky outcropping, apparently devoid of cover.

"Either there is a cave there, or he has gone over the top," whispered Savard. "You circle around to the crest while I remain here. If you jump the cat, I will be able to see him, and if he has gone to den, I will climb straight up from here while you guard from above. We will have him trapped between us."

A driving wind from the western peaks partially blinded Garth as he topped the ridge, but a moment's search revealed no fresh cougar tracks. Looking down, he could barely see a muddle of tracks on a ledge below, and he waved to Savard and pointed to them.

The climb was treacherous, and Savard nearly fell twice before he reached the open end of the narrow ledge. Garth, his weapon ready, watched his burly companion closely, but could see neither tracks nor cougar.

Savard was half turned to question Garth when a snarling, hissing flash of tawny grey reared out of a crevice and straight at Savard. The big woodsman threw up his rifle but was too late. The cat struck him, and both of them tumbled off the ledge and down to the snowpack thirty feet below.

Garth could only watch in astonishment as they struck the snowpack together, the cat on top. Then it slashed once with a forepaw and leapt away. Garth, unable to shoot earlier because of the entangled forms, now took the chance of a snap shot. The cat crumpled in mid-leap, and, as Garth watched, Savard dragged himself to the animal and stabbed it again and again.

His ferocity and blood lust spent, he rolled over and waved

up at Garth.

"Hah! This bastard will kill no more horses. But I have broken my leg in the fall, I think, and my arm is cut pretty bad, too."

Garth motioned him to wait, then began searching for a navigable route by which he could reach Savard and the cat. No sense, he thought, in risking a broken leg of his own at this stage of things.

The biting cold had begun to congeal the blood in Savard's scratches by the time Garth reached the big man, and Garth was more afraid of the cold now than the relatively minor claw wounds. He knew the real danger in them would come from the risk of infection but decided it was preferable to seek shelter before trying to tend the wounds.

The snowpack sloped downward to a small grove of scrub spruce, which to Garth's eye suggested the quickest possible shelter and would be the easiest to reach. The uncertain footing bothered him. He knew he could probably carry Savard, despite the big man's weight and bulk, but he was afraid of falling and doing further damage to the dangerously broken leg.

He could see a whitened shard of bone protruding from Savard's torn legging and knew immediate treatment was a necessity if he didn't want to be dragging a corpse back down the mountain.

"This isn't going to be easy for you," he told Savard. "I am going to try and slide you down to that grove of trees . . . head first. You need to steer with your arms if you can and try to protect that leg as much as you can."

It took half an hour of pulling and sliding to reach the thicket, and another few minutes before Garth could get a decent fire going in the center of it. Shock, by this time, was beginning to take a toll on Savard's strength, and the big man was noticeably shaking.

But he refused to let Garth cut off his leggings so as to get a proper look at the broken leg. "*Mon Dieu,* it is all I have," he said through chattering teeth. "Rather I should take them off and be cold a little more. At least I would have something to wear when we go down the mountain."

Moments later, naked from the waist down, he was bracing his good leg against the base of a small tree and straining to hold himself steady while Garth attempted to manipulate the broken leg back into place. The grating scrunch as it came together sent shivers down Garth's spine, and Savard uttered one piercing moan and then collapsed into a merciful unconsciousness, where he stayed while Garth whittled some splints and washed the wounds with melted snow water before binding the leg and wrapping the big man in every blanket they possessed.

Then he set up the tea pail and set it to brewing. He used compresses of the tea leaves on the claw wounds, pleased that only one of them appeared really severe. It was dark by the time Savard regained consciousness, still shaking from shock but reasonably warm to the touch.

Garth fed him some broth and tea, rebound the wounds, and scrounged enough firewood to get them through the night. He slept in short bursts, waking often to keep the fire going strongly. By morning, Savard's color was looking better, and it was obvious he had recovered from the shock and cold. Also, his evil disposition had returned with a vengeance.

"Well, young one, we have the problem, eh? How are you going to get Savard down this mountain, I wonder."

Garth had been thinking that over during the night, and he was sure there was only one way. "I'm not going to try and carry you, that's for certain," he retorted, drawing a hearty laugh from Savard.

"Nobody has carried Savard since he was a *bébé*. Besides, you are not strong enough."

Garth wasn't about to argue the toss. He swiftly packed their meager camp goods and arranged everything in Savard's pack-sack, then strode over to where the big man lay.

"Turn around so I can hitch this pack on you," he ordered. "I've seen voyageurs half my size carry four hundred pounds on a packboard, and I'm a damned sight stronger than any of them. The only alternative is a travois, and for that we need some decent poles, which up here we do not have. I don't know how your leg is going to take this, but I'm going to try and pack you out, unless you want to crawl down this mountain by yourself."

Savard shrugged his acceptance but pleaded with Garth to at least go back and get the cougar's paws to take with them.

"They won't weigh enough to make a difference, and they will make a nice present for that pretty little squaw, that Climbing Woman," Savard said, innocence in his dark eyes if not in his soul.

Garth didn't know whether to be angry or simply accept the comment as spoken. Even after he had clambered back up the snowpack and gotten the paws, he wasn't sure how he ought to feel.

He added them to the pack, then began the perilous descent with Savard's weight heavy on his shoulders as he probed with his rifle for secure footing. By the time he'd stopped for about the twentieth time to rest, they'd made less than a mile—still descending slowly—and Savard was pale in the face when Garth shrugged him off so he, himself, could get a decent breath.

"We will never make it this way," he gasped. "There has to be an easier way."

Ordering Savard to wait—not that the big man had much choice—Garth moved into a copse of dense spruce and returned after half an hour with a huge, broken piece of tree trunk.

"Aha!" Savard cried in apparent delight. "A toboggan. I must take it all back what I said about you, young Cameron. You're really not that stupid after all."

Garth fought down his temper, partially because he couldn't imagine how a man in such a helpless situation could maintain Savard's arrogance and taunting defiance. Instead, he fought for calm as the two men worked with their knives to shape the shattered timber into something more useful. It wasn't easy, or pretty, but eventually they wound up with something on which he could drag Savard instead of trying to carry him.

The huge piece of tree trunk was clumsy, and one end was so rotten it wouldn't hold the twisted blanket-rope Garth fashioned, but after some practice they began to make real progress. Once they hit the old trail down the ridge, the sled practically moved itself, and they reached the edge of the meadow just before dusk.

Now on more or less level ground, the going grew tougher, if anything. With only half a mile to go, Garth was reluctant to halt, but his burning lungs and near-exhaustion demanded a pause.

"Young Cameron, you are a tougher man than I thought." Savard's voice reached through Garth's panting and wheezing, the noise of his own body making it difficult for Garth to either hear the big woodsman or take in what he was saying.

"And because it is Christmas Eve, I'm think, when all men are supposed to show brotherly love, I am going to tell you something," Savard said, twisting in the snow so he could face Garth directly.

"First, I tell you that your little Climbing Woman, as far as I know, anyway, is still a maiden. That story I tell you before, up on the mountain, that is only to play a little game, eh?

"And now, I'm going to tell you something else. Because you have save the life of Louis Savard, when our truce it is finish in the spring, I am not going to kill you. I will fight you, because I have made that promise to myself long ago. But I am not going

143

to kill you . . . just maybe cripple you a little bit."

Garth, numb with cold and exhaustion from the strain of his ordeal, now began to wonder if he wasn't hearing things. He looked wonderingly at Savard, seeing the fierceness of the big man's dark eyes, and taking in the taunting, sneering chuckle that followed the threat, but it was too weird for him to try and make sense of it all.

Easier for him to turn and trudge off into the gloaming, dragging his enemy along behind him on the makeshift toboggan.

CHAPTER SEVENTEEN

Garth slept through most of Christmas day, rising in the late afternoon to find himself alone in the cabin he'd been sharing with two of the young, unmarried Iroquois men since René had moved out.

Throwing aside his blankets, he was startled to discover that his clothing was all gone, as were the three tanned wolf hides and the cougar paws he'd carried down the mountain while dragging the wounded Savard.

He had no chance to consider the situation, however, before there was a thundering of knocks on the cabin door, and all Garth could do was jump back under his blankets as René bustled in, shouting, "Merry Christmas, *mon ami*," and carrying several bundles.

"Ho-ho-ho," he cried theatrically. "Because I am the only good Catholic in all the camp, they let me say the mass and even play the Saint Nicholas. Actually, I was going to let the girls deliver their own presents to you, but of course you are not dressed quite properly to receive the young ladies, eh?"

Striking a ludicrous pose there on the doorstep, he began to toss the bundles one by one to Garth, describing everything as he did so.

"From Elise, the leggings and moccasins of finest elk hide. And a breechclout that might be a bit . . . over-sized," he said with a wry chuckle. "I'm thinking maybe she is dreaming a little.

"And from Monique, of the long and lovely legs, this splendid elk skin hunting shirt, which you can see she has decorated with the quills of the *Kakwa,* the porcupine. She does good work, this one."

The old man paused for effect, then continued. "Now, let me see . . . ah! Here there is a small package from old René, the voyageur you have travelled with for so long and so far. I think it is a fine cap of prime lynx fur to cover your tender ears. And so . . . Merry Christmas, I say to you again." And out the door he whisked, only to return almost before the door could shut.

"Such a foolish old man I have become. *Mon Dieu,* I forgot the little present from Ilona the Climbing Woman."

And from behind his back he brought a moose hide parka of such exquisite design and decoration that Garth could only stare at the garment, unable to find words for the magnificence of the gift.

The leather had been tanned and smoked using old, rotten birch stumps to bring forth a rich, chocolate coloring. The hood was trimmed with wolverine, the ultimate frost guard.

But the beadwork was what caught the eyes. Using both beads and porcupine quills, Ilona had symbolically depicted Garth, himself—a strong, blond, and bearded young man in combat with a mighty, rearing bull elk.

The man's right arm was bathed in blood, and there was a blanket of crimson flowing down his chest, while the elk, in perfect detail, had a patch of blood flowing down one shoulder to form a wolf's head.

"*C'est magnifique,*" said René, "and all the more so when you consider the clever way she made it."

Pointing to the new and gaily decorated vest on his own small form, he laughingly explained how Ilona had cunningly convinced the other two girls that the vest was for Garth, meanwhile crafting the magnificent parka on the sly.

Garth, only beginning to recover his composure, had begun to stammer out questions, but old René waved them aside and continued his oratory.

"Come on, now. Let us get you all fancied up in your new clothes, or we shall be late for the party. Everybody is over in the old chief's cabin, crowded in like bees in a honey tree. So come on! Everybody is waiting for you, great slayer of mountain lions . . . and I'm getting hungry, me."

And everyone, indeed, was there when the two arrived. Even Savard had been carried to old Wanyandie's cabin for the feast, and was lolling on a pile of furs in one corner, solicitously attended by one of the camp's widows.

A rousing cheer greeted Garth's arrival, and he immediately became the center of a laughing, boisterous crowd, all seeking to shake his hand and thank him for his part in the slaying of the cougar. Savard, too, came in for a share of praise and seemed to accept it with good grace even though his dark eyes held no softness when he looked at Garth.

But silent, in one corner of the room, was a trio of lovely young native women, each with a wolf skin draped like a shawl around her shoulders. Not until the chief had dismissed the throng with much waving of arms and shouting in Iroquois did the three girls flock to Garth like a covey of quail, each planting a kiss on his cheek before retreating again to huddle with their backs to him.

Throughout the evening, women kept scurrying back and forth between the various cabins of the Iroquois encampment, carrying steaming bowls and platters of succulent meats. Most of the men, however, remained in the chief's cabin, drinking vast quantities of a potent brew created from fermented berries.

Between tasting the tender morsels offered him by each passing food carrier, Garth kept attempting to move closer to Ilona, who now sat alone in a far corner of the room. The golden wolf pelt across her shoulders cast rosy hints on her skin as she silently labored to free the claws from the cougar paws.

René had already pointed out to Garth his judicious choice of gifts with which to play Saint Nicholas. "If you would leave everything to old René, you would have no trouble with women," he told his young companion. "I have had more than my share, but never, in all of my life, half the trouble you have had in this winter alone."

Garth gave up trying to navigate a path through the dense crowd, and to avoid telling the story of the lion kill for what seemed to him to be the hundredth time, he slipped out the door.

The chill air quickly combined with the abundance of home brew he'd consumed, serving to speed up the effects. By the time he reached his own cabin, he knew he was thoroughly intoxicated and barely able to navigate.

Head reeling, he threw himself into his blankets and within minutes was snoring gently. He scarcely felt the slim body of the girl as she slipped in beside him but was aroused to a dreamy, half-conscious lust by the capable fingers that slipped beneath his breechclout.

To his groggy mind, the coupling seemed to take forever in a trancelike silence broken only by his own panting and the girl's eventual moans of fulfillment. Drained, he pulled her closer to his body, murmuring Ilona's name drowsily and savoring the sound of it as he did so.

A squalling hiss of anger and the sting of a hand across his face brought him partially awake, but only in time to see a half-naked shadow flit through the open door before it closed with a derisive slam.

"Oh, my good God, now what have I done?" he whispered, struggling to find his clothing in the darkness and hampered by smarting eyes, tearful after the slap. He had to light a candle to see what he was doing, and it was a full fifteen minutes before he was able to slip self-consciously through the door of the chief's home.

Ilona was sitting where he'd last seen her, patiently working at the cougar paws. Elise was busy helping her mother carry trays of food and gave Garth a coy glance as she passed. He didn't immediately see Monique, but when he did locate her, it was with a sinking feeling in his already queasy belly.

Doeskin skirt hiked well up on the thighs of her long, lovely legs, she was sitting in the far corner of the room, laughing into the smirking face of Savard. The big woodsman's dark eyes flashed sardonic amusement when he noticed Garth, but when Monique turned to meet Garth's gaze, her look was hot as hell and cold as the weather outside, all in the same glance.

Sick to his stomach, Garth turned to find himself face to face with Ilona, and the slap mark on his face seemed, to him, to light up like a brand. But she merely smiled demurely, murmured her thanks to him for the present, and, before he could reply, slipped back into the swirling crowd.

He looked back towards Monique, and now there was no question. The glare she sent his way came from two black pools of hatred. Then she turned again to Savard, leaving Garth to stumble from the room, unhappily wiser than before.

Chapter Eighteen

Spring came late to the valley of the Porcupine, heralded by the *suskun yootin,* the melting Chinook winds called snow-eater by the Blackfoot. The warm winds poured down from the crests of the mountains, sometimes clearing entire valleys of accumulated snow virtually overnight.

For Garth Cameron, the time since Christmas had been relatively uneventful, except for the growing tensions provoked by Monique. The long-legged Iroquois beauty continued to join her sister and Ilona in flirting with Garth, but there was no friendliness in her dark eyes when only he could see them, and her flirting had the sting of a bullwhip.

In such moments, her eyes snapped with a fiery hatred, and, if no one else could hear, she would mutter things like, "How is your Peigan slut today, white man? Have you told her yet, or shall I?"

She never said anything else, but it was enough to assure Garth that the episode that occurred during the party was not over—might never be over—and that his drunken dalliance had a price yet to be paid. René, too, had begun to sense trouble brewing. He'd noticed Monique's attitude, and one night was certain he saw Monique sneaking around near the cabin used by Savard.

Mentioning it to Garth one evening in early April, he noted the younger man's obvious discomfort and quickly prodded the entire sordid story from his friend.

"Crazy young bastard! Do you always think with your balls?" he raged. "Why did you not tell me sooner, so we could have worked out a plan, or at least *tried* to work out a plan. In maybe a week, maybe two, we are going to be ready to head south, but do you think that Iroquois slut is going to let you go that easily? These people have very strict rules about such things, my young friend. If all she does is to say you bedded her, they might let you off easily, with a wedding! But if she turns out to be carrying your woods colt . . . or it might be Savard's, for all we know . . . and how do you know she is not, with Savard bedding her every third night? *Mon Dieu,* young Garth . . . they will castrate you and throw you to the wolves."

"Well it isn't as if I planned it, you know? Is it my fault she took advantage of me when I was drunk?" Garth countered, knowing even as he said the words that it was the most pathetic of excuses.

"Of course it is your fault." René's voice reeked of his disgust and anger. "Any man who gets so drunk he doesn't know who is in his bed, he shouldn't be allowed to drink." René then set to concocting a host of schemes, most of them ridiculous, all aimed at saving his young friend from what seemed inevitable— the wrath of a woman scorned.

But it was not René's scheming that saved Garth's skin; it was Elise, the younger Iroquois sister.

The day of their departure had been set for the next morning. It had been decided and approved by the chief, and René was busy rounding up their horses when the door to the Wanyandie cabin flew open, and two clawing, shrieking figures spilled out into the mud.

"Slut! Whore! Pig!" Elise screamed like a cougar in heat, yanking at her sister's hair and trying futilely to kick the taller girl in the stomach. Monique fought back in a grim silence, but it took six men to separate the battling sisters just as René arrived to survey the scene with growing concern.

Demands for an explanation brought the old chief only a sneering silence from his eldest daughter, Monique, but Elise, after a suitable pause for effect, was more than coherent in pouring out a tale of lust and betrayal and sibling rivalry.

Monique, she insisted, had been sleeping with Savard for half the winter but now was growing tired of him and was trying to trap Garth in a web of lies.

"If he belongs to anybody, it is me," she said, then outlined in sordid, embarrassing detail the events of Garth's erotic Christmas nap. She changed only two details—one to make herself the outraged lady of the incident, and the other to free Garth of any and all responsibility.

"He did nothing. He was too drunk!" she shouted in apparent disappointment, then stomped back into her family's cabin amidst jeers of laughter from the dozen spectators who had gathered to watch the performance.

For her part, Monique remained silent, then strode off behind the cabin after the slightest pause in front of Ilona, to whom she whispered only one word: "Bitch."

Ilona shot Garth an unreadable look, then approached René to whisper, "We will go in the morning?"

He nodded, and she twisted her way through the crowd and into the chief's cabin, leaving Garth and René shaking their heads.

Panther-like screams brought Garth wide awake in the half-light of dawn. Confused, at first, he was half-convinced some new cougar had gone mad amongst the pony herd. Running from his cabin when he heard the screams, Garth saw Monique leap astride René's saddle pony, kick the little roan into a full gallop, and charge down the trail to the river.

Garth entered the chief's cabin to find Ilona, bloody from a superficial wound on her left forearm, cradling a dying Elise in her arms, heedless of the blood from both their wounds and crying, "Thank you," over and over again. Elise, raising one hand weakly in the chopping "cut-off" hand signal, murmured, "It is over," then closed her eyes and died.

"She saved my life," Ilona told Garth and later the chief himself. "Monique went . . . mad. She came at me like a mad woman, like an animal, screaming and crying, but I couldn't understand what she was saying, or why. Elise jumped in, trying to save me, and now she's dead—killed by her own sister!"

She fled, then, as if in fear of the crowd that had gathered to the commotion and didn't return to the settlement until late in the afternoon.

The entire camp spent three days seeking Monique after René's horse returned the next morning, wandering along contentedly with a mouth full of new spring grass, but no sign of the girl. It was Garth who found her, hanging by her doeskin dress from a jack pine on a ridge near the river.

Her face was a distorted, blackened mess, but the long legs, even twisted in the agony of her wasteful death, still retained their vivid loveliness. Sick with the bile of his own guilt in the situation, he cut her down, then wrapped the stiffened body in the elk skin shirt she had made for him only months before.

Garth's horse found his own way home, with his rider gazing emptily at the tortured body in his arms. Garth rode into the encampment, handed Monique's body into the arms of an impassive Henri Wanyandie, then turned and rode out again in a grim silence, saying nothing, seemingly seeing no one.

Ilona, glancing inquisitively at René, saw the old voyageur shake his head wearily and mutter, "*Kukwa tuke yimow*—he is sick in his heart."

René left the instant the girl's funeral was over and located Garth four days later, squatting hunched on the bared ridge above the cougar's den. His horse, halter rope trailing and the crude blanket saddle dragging beneath its belly, was grazing in the small meadow below. The youth didn't look up as René approached but stared vacantly into the valley below, as it seemed to René he must have been doing for days.

Speaking softly, as if to a frightened animal, René stepped to the young man's side. Getting no response, he spoke again, more harshly this time, anger creeping beside the concern in his voice.

Garth neither looked up nor spoke in reply . . . merely stared straight ahead like a blind statue.

The old man mumbled to himself briefly in French, then squared his wiry shoulders, stepped to Garth's side, and backhanded him across the face, toppling him over backwards on the rock.

Blood pouring from his nose, mumbling incoherent curses, Garth staggered to his feet, only to collapse on legs cramped beyond use from the length of his vigil. Again and again he tried to stand, to catch and break the monkey-like old man who now sat at a safe distance and smiled scornfully, speaking words Garth couldn't quite understand.

Eventually the roaring in his ears ceased, and he could make out the words, ". . . such a soft young fool you are. What were you going to do, jump off the cliff? Me, I don't think you would have found the nerve.

"For once, please try to listen to old René. I grant you your sorrow. And your guilt. You deserve both, and a good whipping besides. But, my friend, it is not the end of the world.

"You have made the mistake. And somebody else has paid the price. Often it happens in this world. Your time will come, and the price then will be on your own shoulders, and you will have to bear it, but death is for the dead and not the living. You have made the foolishness of a young boy, but you have come here now, alone, to bear your grief and your guilt. Alone, as it should be, for a man.

"No one can blame you for this whole sorry business more than you blame yourself. Now you must go forward and live as a man. Come; we shall go together back to the Iroquois settlement. Monique, she is buried there, among her people as she should be. The time here for mourning, it is over.

And moistness showed in the old man's eyes as Garth broke down, collapsed in a heap on the rocky knoll, and cried and cried and cried.

CHAPTER NINETEEN

Young Daniel Wanyandie, the one they called Tall Colt, met them at the base of the ridge, his pony lathered from heavy riding and words tumbling from his lips in a welter of muddled Iroquois and bits of broken English he'd picked up from Garth over the winter.

René, his Iroquois still far from perfect, had to stop the boy three times in order to have the message clearly understood. Then he threw his hands in the air and shouted to Garth, despite the fact they were only a few feet apart.

"That son-of-a-bitch Savard! The bastard he has taken Ilona during the funeral and he's gone . . . up the river. And here we are, with only one rifle and only one horse that is fit to ride any distance. Come now, young Cameron, we must go quickly back to the settlement and get your weapons and fresh horses for us both."

"Like hell we will," Garth snarled. "Give me your rifle and that spare blanket. I'm going after the bastard right now. The river flows around this ridge to the southwest. I can try to cut him off while you go back for supplies. If we both go back now, it will give Savard a three-day head start. That goddam half-breed bastard! I'll break him in two with my bare hands."

Grasping René's rifle and accoutrements in one hand and the blanket in the other, he kicked his pony so hard it grunted and bounded off southward along the ridge.

René shouted a caution at his friend's departing back, then

turned down the homeward trail after young Wanyandie, nudging the boy's weary pony aside in his scurrying attempts to kick some speed out of his own mount.

The old voyageur's provident ways turned out to be a godsend for Garth. In the borrowed shot pouch were a plentiful supply of flints, a handle-less skinning knife, and a pound of pemmican wrapped in a pouch of moose intestine. His grief-stricken trance over, Garth found himself ravenous, and he ate half the pemmican while charging his pony across the ridge at a full gallop despite the dangerous terrain.

It was five miles, he thought, to the river, but before he'd gone more than one, Garth realized he'd be walking if he pushed the already weary horse any harder. It had not been an easy winter for the Iroquois pony herd, and fresh spring graze was only now starting to emerge. The pony's ribs were visible and the ride far less than comfortable.

Following a series of game trails, dropping steadily downward from the steep side canyons, he rode more than ten miles before he saw the glistening brown water ahead of him. There was an ancient trail he'd heard about from the Iroquois elders that followed the Porcupine River west into the mountains. But with the stream in full flood, he doubted the safety of the fords. Those near the village had been barely passable when he had crossed days earlier.

He was vaguely surprised, then, to find fresh pony tracks headed upstream on the south side. That they belonged to his quarry, he didn't doubt for a moment. The lead pony's tracks were driven deep into the boggy ground, while the tracks of the second mount hardly showed.

His memory skimmed over the myriads of hints René had given him about tracking as he noted also that neither pony seemed to be of any size, which boosted his confidence about catching up to the fleeing Savard. Garth's own mount was winter gaunt, but it was also a large, rangy animal, still capable of carrying his substantial weight. From the look of the tracks, Savard had grabbed up the first ponies he could catch, and neither was of a size to carry the big man without strain.

"No more than a day old," he muttered to himself. "I could catch them by tonight, or tomorrow at the worst."

He had to force himself into camp that night, however, realizing it would be folly to push his tired horse over an uncertain trail in the dark while seeking to gain as much time as he could. Riding at a twisting walk through a stand of low spruce just on dusk, he'd been able to club down two drowsy spruce grouse with his rifle barrel. He gutted them as he rode and later ate them with the remaining pemmican, making only the tiniest of fires when he had to halt for the night.

At sunrise he rode on to find a frothing, leaden torrent at the ford where the South Porcupine joined the main river. Savard's tracks showed he'd turned up the smaller stream, likely fearing to try the risky ford.

Garth's pony also feared the frothy current, rearing in panic at every attempt made to ride him into the ford. Then, knowing it was a long chance, but sure Savard would return to the main trail somewhere ahead, Garth abandoned the pony, loaded his scant supply of provisions on his back, and crossed the torrent on a fallen log. His knees trembled when he jumped to safety on the far side, but after two miles of jogging along the trail, he found the gamble had paid off. Clear in the mud of the main trail now were the tracks of Savard's two mounts, showing the big man had crossed higher up and then had to turn back downstream to hit the trail again. It meant Garth might have gained significant ground, and in this rugged terrain he reckoned he could make as good time on foot as Savard could on horseback.

Refreshed by the discovery, Garth increased his pace, trundling along in the sort of smooth dog-trot a southern Plains Indian could maintain for days. Alert to each root and hummock in the trail, and watching cautiously for any possible ambush, he'd covered another four miles when nature took a hand in the game.

Above him, the sky turned leaden as a spring blizzard surged over the mountains. Within minutes, the ground was white with sodden snow, and within the hour, Garth was slipping and sliding in ankle-deep slush. It was like running in sand . . . the harder he worked, the slower he seemed to travel. When a slip narrowly missed sending him into the river a hundred feet below, he realized the insanity of it and slowed to a long-striding walk.

But the snow grew deeper with virtually every stride, and Garth, sweating from his early exertions, was beginning to feel the chill. Certain the snow would slow down Savard's ponies, he had to hope they, too, would be stopped by the spring blizzard.

He made a snug camp deep in a spruce thicket and well away from the main trail. With nothing to eat, he had no need to build a fire. He drank a small quantity of snow melted in his hands, knowing it was risky but having no choice. Curled up in the blanket on a bed of spruce boughs, he slept fitfully. By mid-afternoon, the snow had ceased to fall, so Garth shrugged himself awake and once again took the trail west along the river.

He saw Savard's fire from almost a mile away, a tiny red glow like a single coal. Only his height on a ridge sticking out into the adjacent valley had allowed him to see it at all, he realized. Two steps to the right or left, and it disappeared.

It was nearly full dark already, and it took him two hours to get within sight of Savard's camp. The ponies were tethered in a small meadow, and Savard and Ilona were crouched by the fire under a jack pine on the edge of the meadow. It was impossible for him to tell in the waning light whether Ilona was tied, or tethered.

Garth began circling the meadow, deep in the timber but always within sight of the horses. They were his worst danger, and he knew it. If Savard had taken Indian ponies that were unfamiliar with Garth, the slightest smell of a stranger might spook them enough to warn the half-breed.

Even as that thought crossed Garth's mind, a shifting eddy of wind took his scent into the meadow, causing the smaller horse to perk its ears inquiringly. Garth halted in his tracks, and a moment later the pony lowered its head and continued grazing.

Without the snow, he'd have been unable even to see the horses, Garth knew. With the cloudy skies, Savard and Ilona were visible only as shifting shadows around the tiny glow of the fire.

Noise from the huge waterfall a half-mile downstream covered any sound he made, but each time Garth tried to sneak within rifle range, one pony or the other would begin to fidget. Fearing to push his luck in the darkness, he retreated and curled up in his blanket beneath a pine tree, determined to wait until morning before he made a move.

The wind from the mountains changed for the worse overnight, losing the gentleness of the *suskun yootin,* the snow-eating Chinook winds from the far, high west. These new winds were more local, and when the sky first began to lighten, it was a nearly-frozen Garth Cameron who managed to sneak within gunshot range of the sleeping Savard camp.

He'd determined, during a near-sleepless, shivering night, that the safest way to deal with the huge and unquestionably dangerous woods boss would be to shoot the man as he lay in his blankets.

"The hell with fair play," he'd muttered through chattering teeth. "I saved the bastard's life once, and look what that accomplished."

The rising light of dawn, however, presented a new dimension to the problem. Garth couldn't determine with certainty which of the blanket-wrapped figures was Savard. One certainly appeared larger than the other, but the stakes were too high, he felt, for him to take any risk. Trembling with cold and increasingly fearful the grazing ponies would notice him and give an alarm, he waited and shivered for another half-hour before one of the figures stirred.

Swiftly, Garth cocked his rifle but was unable to shoot for another five minutes as the shrouded figure tossed back and forth without rising to give him a clear view of his target. But then an all-too-familiar black beard poked up out of the blankets as Savard reared up on one elbow and looked around the camp.

Rock steady, Garth squeezed the trigger, heard the hammer strike, but the powder fizzed out in the pan. Roaring a curse upon all such rifles, he leapt to his feet and charged toward Savard, drawing his knife and holding it low for a slashing, upward stroke at the first opportunity.

But, chilled as he was, Garth couldn't move fast enough. Before he'd gone even ten steps, Savard had rolled from his blankets and had his own knife at Ilona's throat.

"Look, my sweet, your young boyfriend has come to play with Savard," he said, never taking his gaze from where Garth had halted, uncertain, but still ready to take what action he could.

"Throw down your knife, Cameron, or I'll cut her throat like a chicken. Did I not say before that we would settle this thing between us without weapons? Put it down now, or the prize in this little game will be one dead Peigan squaw!"

Numbly, Garth dropped the knife. And waited, so sick at

heart he thought he might be sick to his stomach.

The burly half-breed grinned fiercely through his beard as he noted Garth's weakened condition. Garth was visibly shivering, and it was the cold, rather than his anger, that was causing it.

Dragging Ilona with him, Savard moved in a circle to pick up Garth's abandoned rifle, having obviously noted that Garth was otherwise unarmed. Keeping his own weapon cocked and ready, Savard motioned Garth to a log across the fire from him and ordered Ilona to prepare a meal.

"It would not be a fair fight now," Savard said with an evil grin. "Not with you so cold and Savard without his breakfast. Come now. Be a good boy and eat with us. Then we will go down and play by the river, eh?"

It was the man's astonishing calm that frightened Garth more than anything. Without the impetus of his own anger, Savard loomed even larger than normal, and the older man's confidence was a weapon in itself.

Numbly cursing his own ineptness, Garth struggled through the effort of consuming the boiled meat and bannock prepared by the frightened girl, who hardly even glanced at him. When the meal ended, he was astounded to see Savard lean back against a convenient tree, stoke his pipe, and begin smoking as Ilona finished her own breakfast.

But never did the huge Métis relax his vigilance, and never was there a moment when either Garth or Ilona wasn't threatened by the only loaded gun remaining in the camp.

"Well, young one, it has been a long trail," Savard said. "How did you catch us so quickly, and on foot? It must be that you forded at the old crossing. *Mon Dieu!* I will wager you rode your horse to death also, eh? You are a persistent young fool, I shall give you that. But . . . so stupid.

"Do you not know there is no man—red, white, or even Métis—who can defeat Louis Savard? It is known all along the rivers from Montreal to Rocky Mountain House. They do not call me *le Carcajou*—the wolverine—because I am gentle, you must realize."

Pausing to relight the pipe with a casualness that was in itself a threat, he continued his monologue with a flash of teeth beneath the ursine beard.

"Such a pity, really, that we must fight on such a miserable day. And with nobody but this puny little squaw to watch, *non?* But it must be done. You have been in my way too long already. You are like a mosquito, always buzzing around."

Savard laughed, but it wasn't a pleasant sound. "Since you have been so good as to clumsily wander into my camp like this, I will do the favor I once promised back in the Iroquois settlement. I will not kill you, just break your bones enough to that you must lie still and watch while I bed with your woman. When you see how much she enjoys Louis Savard, you will know what a waste of time it has been for you to trouble me."

The gigantic half-breed leapt to his feet with the grace of a predatory animal, swatted Ilona casually across the head with his rifle barrel, then tossed the weapon aside even as she fell. "Come now," he said, "Let us begin this."

Startled, Garth leapt to his own feet as he saw Ilona slump unconscious to the snow. He needed no second invitation. Cursing, he charged at Savard in a blind rage, only to be brushed aside in one sweeping, bear-like blow.

Garth was thrust head-first into a jack pine but quickly recovered and again leapt at his opponent. This time he was thrown to the ground with another casual wave of the bigger man's enormous hand. Slower to get up, he had to face the grim reality that Savard was only playing . . . for the moment.

Cautiously, Garth slipped into a crouch and circled around the tiny campfire, always keeping Savard in sight. Garth's breath came in short, panting bursts, but Savard moved silently, his breath a patient whistle through the brush of his dense, black beard.

He feinted twice, easily drawing Garth off balance, then gathered him into an iron grip that threatened Garth's ribs. Savard's shout was still ringing in his ears when Garth realized he must break free or perhaps lose the fight before it had hardly begun.

He stomped down hard on Savard's instep then butted him in the face with his head. Blood streamed from a crushed nose as Savard shouted curses. He released Garth and paused to wipe at his own face. Garth took advantage of the respite to regain his wind, feeling the strain on his ribs.

Crouching, he grasped a small stick from the fire pit and threw it at the burly Savard, then followed with a plunging assault that drove the big man backwards toward the river. Savard grunted with the impact, then spread his arms in an attempt once again to squeeze his opponent into submission.

Garth, having learned from the first mistake, slipped under the other man's grasping arms and tried to punch Savard in the belly. The effort nearly cost him a knee in the groin, but he managed—if only barely—to turn the blow with his thigh, which immediately went partially numb from the striking knee.

Savard grasped Garth by one sleeve, yanking at his arm in another attempt to bring Garth in reach of Savard's murderous hands. Knowing his only hope lay in evasive action, Garth allowed himself to be carried toward Savard, then turned to throw himself forward with the momentum of the bigger man's pull. Smashing an elbow into Savard's chest, he pushed the burly half-breed closer to the edge of the swift-flowing, ice-rimmed river. The attack landed Savard on his back within inches of the shore, with Garth sliding off to one side, where he halted in a gasping crouch.

Near exhaustion, Garth saw that Savard was breathing heavily as well. He and Savard slipped cautiously on the treacherous riverside stones, risking a fall with every stride, every move and counter-move. Neither could gain any advantage, both of them barely able to keep their footing.

Seeing Savard slip halfway to his knees, Garth launched a driving attack. Halfway through the rush, he realized it was a ruse and tried desperately to turn aside. But his footing failed him, and he slid into the larger man's knees, out of control but quick enough to grasp Savard's ankles in a bid to bring the bigger man down with him. It partially worked. Savard fell backwards into the icy waters of the river, but he maintained a grip on Garth's hair as he fell and dragged Garth in with him.

For what seemed like hours, they rolled and thrashed in the current, first one on top and then the other. Numbed by the cold, neither could get a decent grip for long enough to gain any significant advantage, but Savard's superior strength was beginning to tell.

Garth had learned some boxing as a child, and he came to his feet long enough to drive a smashing blow to Savard's bearded chin, only to find the beard gave his opponent too much protection. But he had little other choice, so he continued to aim blows at Savard's eyes and nose, especially, and the few that landed began to have an effect.

Savard was a brawler, at his best when he could put his huge hands on an opponent and use his superior strength to advantage. Faced with Garth's flickering punches to his face, he began to blunder like a befuddled bear beset by bees, skidding on the slippery rocks and grasping clumsily at the hard-thrown punches.

Garth paused, shaking with exhaustion and cold, then plunged once more toward Savard, whose face was scarlet with blood that streamed from his flattened nose and the cuts on both cheekbones.

Savard seemed equally exhausted, so Garth pitted everything on the chance of scoring strokes to the big man's eyes in a bid to blind him and give Garth some chance of victory. But a slimy, egg-shaped rock turned under his foot, and he found himself stumbling straight into the half-breed's grasp.

Savard grabbed Garth by the hair, dragged him within reach, and then, in a single, herculean effort, swung Garth around and raised him high into the air. Grasped by neck and crotch, Garth could do nothing to save himself as Savard pivoted and flung him across a large rock jutting up from the current.

He landed with the edge of the rock across his kidneys and remained conscious only long enough to feel himself sliding from the rock into the rushing midstream current.

Savard, panting with his efforts, fell to his own knees in the river. Shaking the water from his shaggy hair and beard, he rose slowly upright and stood silent, watching Garth's unconscious body floating face up in the water, headed for the hundred-foot waterfall less than a quarter-mile downstream.

"*Bon chance.* Let the water take him," Savard muttered. "I said I would not kill him, and I have not. Damn, but that was a fight. The young one, he was tougher than I think he would be."

Still staggering, clumsy in his movements, he stumbled ashore and drank a quart of steaming tea straight from the kettle. Only then did he turn with a glance to where Ilona was struggling to reach her own feet, still dazed from the blow he'd inflicted on her with the rifle barrel.

Savard's arousal was a hangover from the violence of the fight, and his instinct was to slake the urge physically, to violate the innocence he knew she possessed. He strode forward and grasped Ilona by the neck of her tunic, lifting her up to face him.

"Now it is your turn, little Climbing Woman," he said. "It is past time you find out what a real man is all about."

Ilona merely stared at him blankly, her dark eyes void of expression or understanding. She swayed in his grasp, would have fallen again were it not for his grip on her tunic. Then, for only a moment, something approaching comprehension floated into existence in her eyes, and Savard recoiled when it seemed they were his sister's eyes, that it was Francine gazing at him in her innocence.

"*Sacré,*" he snarled, then released her tunic and let her fall at his feet, limp as a rag doll and about as appealing. She collapsed without a sound, utterly at his mercy, vulnerable. Maybe too vulnerable.

Now he faced a choice he hadn't expected. He knew Ilona to be a woman of some spirit and had looked forward to the pleasures of breaking that spirit slowly, deliberately, at his leisure. There would be little pleasure to be gained from taking advantage of her while in this condition, although he was tempted. Plus, his pleasure would be lessened since Garth could not be forced to watch and suffer from the sight.

But . . . Francine's image refused to leave him, gnawed at his conscience even as hunger gnawed at his empty belly. He was hurting from his battle, and also hungry . . . then unexpectedly ravenous. And with the waning of his exertions, he was cooling off rapidly. He stood silent for a moment, then began to turn in circles, his eyes roaming from the fallen girl at his feet to the fire and the camping gear nearby . . . his blankets, and the firewood he'd insisted they gather the evening before. Warmth! It became more important than satisfying a lust that had lost all flavor.

It was the work of only moments to boost the fire up to a welcoming, warming blaze, then make more tea and begin slicing the remains of their meat into thick strips to be cooked. He might have to hunt again later, but it was enough for now. The girl could go hungry. She didn't need to be well fed for his purposes.

He threw Ilona's blanket over her where she lay, then reconsidered and tied her feet in improvised but effective hobbles of rawhide thong, with a slip-knot he could release when the time was right, which he expected would be soon. She couldn't stay unconscious forever and when she awoke would be able to move around, to do the woman's work of the camp, but escape would be impossible. And when he did want her, one yank on her rawhide hobbles and his own access would be ensured. She would keep, and would be more enjoyable, he thought, once he had a full stomach and was warm and dry. There would be as much pleasure for him in the sheer anticipation of what was to come, and time would be a factor in that.

He wanted her body, although his taste ran more to the long-legged leanness of the Iroquois woman, Monique. But Ilona offered a different challenge, and it would be the taste of her fear, the flavor of her eventual submission, that he would savor the most.

He tried to convince himself of that as he ate, casually watching her, wishing his mind would stop seeing his sister Francine whenever Ilona turned her head just . . . so. A conscience, he thought, was irrelevant. It would fade, in time, surely.

There was time for that. It would be a long trail back to the North Saskatchewan. By the time they got there, the little Climbing Woman would be willing to climb whatever Savard demanded of her.

CHAPTER TWENTY

Garth Cameron struck a midstream rock as he went over Kakwa Falls, a collision that first hammered his back and then his left ankle. He had no recollection of grabbing at a huge, floating log when he surfaced in the swirling waters a hundred feet below, but once he'd grabbed onto the log he allowed it to keep him afloat as it surged below and then behind the curtain of the falling waters.

In high water, the immense cavern beneath the falls was impossible to see into except from one precarious location outside. Inside, the cavern was almost magical . . . an imposing cathedral of coal-blackened walls and a large bench stacked with driftwood from earlier, higher floods.

Garth was too exhausted to be impressed by the beauty of it since he'd barely managed to heave himself against the rock bench as his log surged past in the whirlpool. He hung there, gasping with the exertion, before he gained sufficient strength to haul himself up out of the icy water.

Barely conscious, but instinctively groping to move himself away from the water's edge, he crawled back into the cavern and collapsed. The light was failing when he eventually regained consciousness, shaking with the cold and wracked by burning pain in his ankle and lower back. It was all he could do to move at all, but he knew it was a matter of move or die. Not a good swimmer at the best of times, he realized he had no hope in his present condition of trying to swim out through the whirlpool that mocked him.

The cavern was partially filled with mist from the falling curtain of water, but the sight of the mounds of driftwood brought immediate thoughts of a fire to his clouded mind.

He fumbled in the soaking bullet pouch still strapped about his waist and found four rifle flints, a bit of oil-soaked buckskin that once had held pemmican, but no dry punk or anything else he might use to start a fire. But there was that broken skinning knife, a weapon without a hilt, but a weapon of steel. And he had flints!

He crawled over to the nearest pile of more-or-less dry driftwood and desperately scrounged around until he found some rotten wood he could break up in his hands and then pulverize with the knife blade. He had to remind himself to stay calm and steady as he formed a small pile of tinder, praying against all logic that it might be dry enough despite the moisture in the air. It took him what seemed like an hour before he was properly positioned over the materials, trying to strike sparks from the knife blade with one of the small rifle flints.

He lost the first one; it flicked from his clumsy, icy fingers and disappeared as if by magic. The second one struck sparks, but by then the punk had dampened in the mist and would no longer take the sparks.

Garth knew he must have fire, and soon, or succumb to the chill and icy damp that seemed to penetrate his very soul. He scrambled deeper into the piles of driftwood, found another chunk of rotten birch, and cautiously crumbled it on the driest piece of rock he could reach. Several minutes of patient scraping with the flint gained him a miniscule, smoldering coal in the midst of the pile, and an eternity of soft, careful puffs upon it started a minute flame.

An hour later, he lay in relative comfort against the far wall of the cavern, sheltered and warming steadily with the reflection from a good-sized fire between himself and the swirling, misting wall of falling water.

Moving was laborious, but possible despite his injuries, and he managed to get his buckskin garments hung up to dry on makeshift racks of driftwood, and although he despaired of them ever totally drying out in the constant swirling mist inside the cavern, he thought the smoke would clear the worst of the moisture out.

He'd bound his swollen ankle in strips of buckskin, torn from the hem of his hunting shirt with his teeth and the broken skinning knife. A check of his ribs revealed severe bruising but no sign of any broken bones. His kidney region was sore to the touch, and he found it hard to bend over without shooting pains, but he'd already found his piss un-bloodied, and he was gradually responding to the fire's life-giving warmth.

Hunger now became a major concern. He anticipated there might be fish in the river, perhaps even in this large pool beneath the falls, but he had little in the way of potential fishing gear and even less in the way of improvisation, with neither line nor hooks.

Lethargic with the warmth from the fire, he drifted into sleep. He dreamed of huge elk steaks and roasted geese until he woke up again to a sputtering fire and, even worse, a debilitating hunger. He stirred up the flames and added several large chunks of driftwood, idly wondering how long the supply would last. Then he noticed the black, coal-streaked walls of the cavern and took new hope.

Using a strong branch that had washed into the cavern but had yet to dry and rot, he managed to pry several chunks of coal from the walls and fed them to the surging flames. The coal was impure and burned sporadically, but it gave off a reassuring glow that promised he'd have fewer problems with heat than with his lack of food.

Hunger had become a ceaseless, gnawing animal in his belly, and he again had to consider his limited options. Scrounging again through the bullet pouch, he discovered the oily pouch that had once held pemmican.

"It won't make much of a meal, but better than eating my moccasins, I suppose—although I wouldn't be the first," he muttered.

Using a green stick, he slowly toasted the pemmican pouch over the coals and, upon first tasting it, almost discarded the idea. "Shit, that's what it tastes like," he muttered, but knowing it was all he was likely to find for some time, he managed to choke it down and—more important—keep it down.

The warm, slightly greasy leather made slow eating, but once he got it into his stomach, it reduced the gnawing hunger enough that he once again drowsed into a fitful sleep. The crude coal he'd scraped from the cavern walls kept the fire going well, and he stayed relatively warm right through until morning, when he had to rouse himself and add more fuel to the dwindling flames.

This time he awoke with a growing, gnawing apprehension about Ilona's fate in the hands of Savard and began plotting his own future. Struggling to keep the weight off his injured ankle, he began a crawling search of the cavern beneath the falls, in hopes of finding some route by which he could reach the river bank and make his way back to the campsite.

The fire was rebuilt, and he chewed listlessly on a thong cut from his hunting shirt as he probed with a stick and tried to see around the misting waterfall that curtained off the entire cavern entrance.

With his crippled ankle, he knew any attempt to swim free of the whirlpool would be impossible, but on both sides of the cavern, the high water swamped any other possible routes to freedom.

He was peering out the south side of the water curtain when he spied René clambering across the rocks to the thrashing waters outside. Garth shouted again and again, but the thunder of the falls drowned out his puny voice. He could not rouse the little voyageur's interest in crossing the slick rock face that bounded the waterfall's edges at that point. He saw René point across the stream and yell something, but he couldn't figure out who his friend was trying to communicate with.

As René started back downstream, Garth became desperate. He glanced at the smoking fire and saw his only possible hope of attracting René's attention.

Grasping the longest and most charcoaled pieces of smoking driftwood from the edges of the fire, he crawled quickly back to the edge of the cavern and tried to fling them out through the falling curtain of water.

With the first two, he was dismally unsuccessful. They bounced off the falling waters and back into the cavern, where they bobbed back to the surface as if laughing at him. Cursing, Garth scrambled back to the fire, grabbed two more large chunks and tried again to throw them through the falling water so that they might float to the surface outside.

He could no longer see René but hoped if one of the charcoaled logs floated downstream, or even traveled to the edges of the eddy outside, the sharp-eyed voyageur would perhaps notice it. Possibly. Maybe. Hopefully.

Twisting into an awkward, left-handed position, he managed to throw the larger of the two chunks out through the curtain, but as he watched, groaning with frustration, it bobbed to the surface right there in front of him—inside the cavern—obviously caught in the same undertow that had brought Garth, himself, to an imprisoned safety the day before.

Angered, he flung the second piece of burned wood higher and harder, through the edge of the water curtain and against the rocky bank outside. He saw it bounce off the rocks twice before landing back in the side current and heading off downstream.

Encouraged, he grabbed up two more smoking brands, pausing this time to add more branches to the dwindling fire. Again, he was able to bounce the smoking wood off the rocky poolside edge. Meanwhile, he shouted as loud as he could in what he considered was probably a useless effort to gain René's attention.

One more attempt and he was out of decent-sized smoking brands and shivering from the cold and damp. Disconsolate, he pushed the fire together again and added some lumps of coal. Then he leaned against the warm rocks close to the blaze and hoped to regain his strength.

In a panic that René would never find him, he was seriously considering an attempt to swim out of the cavern, if he could, but exhaustion claimed him, and he once again drifted into a restless slumber.

Dreams of Savard and the fight brought him to a thrashing wakefulness that seemed almost a dream in the shifting half-light around him. The tracings of coal seams were like ghostly writing in the glow from the fire, and for a moment he thought he must be hallucinating.

The roiling whirlpool below the rock shelf was dark, eerie, and mystical, but he half thought it might be less violent than it had been when he'd emerged from it. Was there some chance, he wondered, that the rains had stopped higher upstream in the river, and the immense falls would shrink enough to give him a way out?

He crawled closer to the edge of the rock shelf and studied the current, not for the first time wishing he was a better swimmer. Even without his injured ankle, in his weakened condition he knew it would be a huge risk to try and escape his water-formed prison.

He was turning away, seeking yet again the comfort of the fireside, when the surface of the pool divided and Ilona slithered like an otter onto the rock shelf beside him, gasping for breath and naked as the day she was born.

CHAPTER TWENTY-ONE

Ilona's loss of consciousness had been partly a ruse, the only weapon she had, given the circumstances. Her head rang with pain, and her vision was vibrating into double and triple images when Savard snatched her up like an oversized doll after his victory over Garth.

She knew what would come next, and neither feared it nor allowed it to concern her all that much. Considering what she had endured at the hands of Mad Wolf and the Cardinal brothers, it could be no surprise that the burly Savard would now take her as a prize of battle. And then . . . ?

Then, she knew, he might take her along with him back to the Saskatchewan, using her as he pleased . . . to do the cooking and to warm his blankets and satisfy his lusts. He would not, she knew, return her to Rocky Mountain House. That almost certainly would provoke a riot amongst her father's friends and the men of David Thompson, who hated Savard like poison. It might even be dangerous for him to keep her at the Hudson Bay Company's Acton House, assuming he still was welcome there. The two posts were too close together for him to take that risk. Maybe.

But one thing was certain . . . Savard was too big and too strong for her to resist his physical approach, and too much of a brute to be appealed to with reason. The fact that she had yet to know a man *in that way* would only offer him a new element of challenge, and she could imagine no gentleness in the circumstance.

She retreated into herself as the big woodsman rolled back her eyelid and grunted his dissatisfaction with her apparent swoon and made sure she stayed limp as he lashed her ankles into the improvised hobble.

He had to be exhausted after the battle, she thought. Had to be! At any rate, he hadn't noticed he had dumped her squarely on the knife Garth had dropped before the fight began. If Savard would only sleep, now . . . and if she didn't freeze to death before he did sleep . . .

Ilona's frigid fingers inched toward the knife on which she lay, but her slit-eyed gaze was locked on the blanket-wrapped form of the black-bearded Savard. He slept restlessly, tossing and turning and snoring and groaning, and with every alteration in his rhythm she halted her hand in its chilly journey to retrieve the knife.

Exactly how she could use the weapon wasn't clear in her befuddled mind. She would need time to reach down and free her feet from his hobbles. She would need time to ensure she could actually reach Savard without waking him. She would need time . . . and time was both her enemy and her possible salvation.

It had been what seemed like hours since Savard abandoned her after her feigned swoon, but Ilona knew how time could stretch out when abetted by cold and fear. And she suffered both.

Her fingers touched the blade, honed to a razor edge, but she was too cold. She couldn't feel the icy steel sufficiently to be sure if she was touching the sharp side or the blunt topside. A wrong move now would gain her only bloodied fingers, making her situation all the more precarious.

It took all her patience to release the blade, to tuck her fingers instead up against the minimal warmth of her body. If she could thaw them enough, she could move them. If she could move them *properly*, she could pick up the knife without slicing off a finger or otherwise harming herself. If she could . . .

Savard rolled over, grunting, snuffling in his sleep like a hog at the trough. Like the pig he was! And now he had only to open his dark, evil eyes to be staring straight at her. Afraid that her own gaze would draw his attention, she looked away, praying that he might turn back over again. She could risk moving while his back was turned, but when all he need do was open his eyes, it was too risky despite the necessity. She lay there, helpless and made more so by the situation and the cold, trying to watch him without looking directly at him, trying to summon up sufficient strength to move swiftly, quietly, effectively.

Then he turned over again, his back to her once more, and she relaxed, cutting off her own sigh of relief lest that rouse him. Again, she glanced at the fire, the hobbled ponies, her apparently sleeping enemy. She grasped the knife, found the hilt by good luck as much as anything else, and slithered herself into a bow so as to reach the hobbles on her ankles.

The rawhide was tight, hardened by drying since he'd tied the hobbles, but she worked slowly, precisely. It wasn't easy, not least because she needed to keep her attention as much on Savard as on the lashings she was trying to sever.

And then—it was done. She felt the hobbles give, knew that her first hurdle had been conquered. It was like a breath of fresh air to her befuddled mind, and she could see properly again, think again, try to plan . . .

Except that before she'd got that far, her enemy rolled up to his feet and stood over her like a ferocious, freshly-wakened grizzly, sleep-spit drooling from his mouth as he swayed there, silent but no less threatening.

"Get up!" The order was harsh and demanding, but even as the words left his mouth, Savard was turning away, moving to bring in the horses. He seemed to have forgotten the hobbles he'd placed on her, and Ilona was so stunned by the luck that she almost looked down to see if she'd imagined them.

Then she had to kick away the remains of the slashed thongs so that she could move herself into the expected tasks of breaking camp, hoping Savard would continue his forgetfulness until—

"Come and help with this saddle." He gave her the order brusquely, over his shoulder, as he fumbled, his left side weakened from the fight with Garth. His face still awash with blood, his nose little more than a flattened lump of bloody tissue between two blackened and bloodied eyes, he looked more animal than human.

Ilona kept the knife concealed as she sidled over and bent down to take the other side of the saddle, but as soon as Savard began to lift his side, she dodged beneath it and drove the knife into him with all the strength she could manage.

Before he could react, she slid it out and repeated the assault, then fled, dodging past her captor, the falling saddle, the piled-up camp gear. Headed . . . anywhere she could find the room to flee, anywhere she could make her chilled, cramped body and legs carry her.

She scampered down the trail toward the falls but momentarily halted to chance one quick look at the campsite . . . where she saw Savard, gasping with pain and surprise, slumped over the now-discarded saddle, already greasy with his blood.

Ilona ran for half a mile along the high trail beside the river before caution overtook her panic and she began to take stock of her situation. She fully expected Savard to follow her, if he lived, and with native cunning she began seeking ways to cover her trail.

The narrow, twisted track through the pines was muddy from melted snow, but most of the surrounding bench was still buried beneath the old snows of winter. To stick with the trail, she knew, meant leaving tracks that the wily woods boss could follow without slowing his pony below a canter. But to leave the trail, either by going up to the crowning ridge top or down to the raging, spring-swollen river of the porcupine, would mean slower going for her and perhaps even easier tracking for her enemy.

She was well below the falls after a cautious descent of the slippery trail when she noticed during a pause for breath the faintest sound of a horse moving towards her from even further downstream. Not Savard, then . . . but who? Ducking quickly from the muddy trail, she slipped into a heavy copse of pine and burrowed under the lower branches of one tree as she waited to see what new enemy might be on the move.

The clop of pony hooves grew slowly more distinct as she shivered beneath the branches. But still she saw nothing until the horse stepped out almost on top of her—and riderless.

She lay unmoving, scenting a trap but unable to figure out precisely where the danger might come from. The pony passed almost out of her hearing, leaving only silence. Her keen ears could detect no other sound in the still, heavy forest.

Then she heard a faint chuckle from behind her and rolled over in terror to see old René, leaning casually on his rifle and watching her.

"Aha, so the Climbing Woman now becomes a hiding rabbit in the deep timber?" he whispered. "If that pony of mine didn't have such a good nose, I would have ridden right past you. But he warned me in time. That pony, he sure doesn't like the scent of an Indian, even a pretty little one like you.

"And so, let us make some tea, and you can tell me what happened to my young friend Garth and that bastard Savard. Here . . . you begin the fire, and I'll go and catch up that scrawny horse before he makes it to the waterfall, eh?"

René tossed a bag of fire makings to the still-shaking girl and turned away to catch up the pony he could even now hear walking quietly along the trail below them. Striding quickly to the muddy trail, he caught up the pony and turned to find Ilona tight behind him, fire-bag in hand.

"Garth . . . Savard has killed him, I think," she said in a rushing mix of Peigan and English. "But maybe he is still alive, and we must go quickly and see. I think I killed Savard, but we must be cautious. I stabbed him twice in the belly but he may already be out there hunting for me. He will come from upstream, and it is so muddy on the trails, so many tracks . . ."

René quickly got the rest of the story from Ilona, then lifted her to the pony's back and started off ahead along the trail back upriver. Ever cautious about Savard, he also kept a close eye on the frothing river below them for any sign of Garth or his body.

He found no sign of either man.

They reached Savard's campsite just on dusk, finding it empty of life. Savard had gone, leaving much of his gear behind but taking both of the ponies. All the signs told them he was hurt— and badly. Where he had fallen beside the saddle, the ground was black with blood, and strips of cloth near the fire indicated he'd been making bandages.

René directed Ilona to stay and make camp, then jogged off along the trail left by the giant half-breed. It was child's play to follow. Savard hadn't bothered to try and follow the girl but had headed upriver to the crossing, then struck off northward to where René believed there was another trail that led west into the mountains.

He returned to the camp, heaped the fire high, and, after a

brief meal, set off downstream along the slippery rocks in search of any sign of Garth. Ilona begged to accompany him, but he ordered her to eat and rest.

"You are too exhausted to be any help, and it might end up with you, too, in the river," he said. Then he scurried off before she could think to mount an argument. He didn't return until nearly midnight, soaked to the waist and shivering so badly with the cold that his teeth chattered.

"I find nothing," he said. "And it would be stupid to thrash around down there in those rocks without light. *Sacré!* Three times, I almost joined Garth in that devil of a river."

In the morning, they took turns—one leading the horse along the slick river trail while the other rock-hopped and slithered and slid along the dangerous edge of the water. The weather was beginning to come good again, and, although the *suskun yootin,* the snow-eating winds, didn't return, spring was noticeably on the way.

"So long as it doesn't start to rain again higher up," René cautioned. "If that happens we might lose every crossing that exists. And young Cameron, wherever he is . . . I cannot think about that, me."

When they reached the crest of the falls, where the current surged across rocks before plunging into the swirling eddy that roiled and boiled beneath the curtain of the waters, René found one possible place where one of them might be able to cross the river. But not both, and certainly not the horse.

"You should do this," he said. "You are younger and more spry than old René, and it will mean we can search back along both sides of the river."

He and Ilona had both been frustrated by not being able to see into the riverbank brush and cover on the other side, thinking that Garth might have gotten himself out of the waters and might be there, somewhere, hidden from their view.

"It will be harder to get down on that side," Ilona pointed out. "The trail is here on this side for a reason." As she spoke, she was edging her way to the lip of the drop-off, leaning dangerously out in a bid to see the bottom.

"I am thinking you might be right," he replied. "Anyway, there is a good crossing not far below the falls, but if he has gone over this, I don't think we ever find him, and certainly not alive."

"I do not think he is here above the falls," Ilona said, speaking bluntly as, it seemed to René, her heart demanded she do. He realized she had to *try* to find Garth, alive or dead, and was determined to die trying if that was what it took.

René felt exactly the same way but led the pony down the steep trail with somewhat less optimism. Both he and Ilona were tired and less than hopeful when they reached the bottom, but, after only the briefest of respites, Ilona found her way to the downstream crossing and a few hours later was waving to René across the shimmering curtain of the high Kakwa Falls.

He had already scouted out the banks on his own side but paralleled her as she moved along the dangerously slippery rocks of the shoreline. Communication was almost impossible except by sign language. The roaring waters caught up their words and flung them into nothingness.

Ilona's side of the river allowed her to move in slightly closer than René could manage, but to do so was far more dangerous, except that it allowed her to clamber up beside the roiling eddy. She couldn't see past the waterfall itself, but below her it was clear the falling waters had caused a back-thrust that must have undercut the rock for some distance.

Her attention focused on René, she caught a movement out of the corner of her eye. Something long and dark-colored that spurted out of the falling curtain of waters but fell quickly and was immediately drawn in under the falls again.

She waved at René, who apparently hadn't seen whatever it was, and tried to tell him in gestures what she'd seen. It was like talking to a tree, she thought, her frustration serving only to make matters worse.

Until it happened again, and this time she knew that both of them had seen the half-burned chunk of log spew out into the current and spin up against the bank, almost at René's feet.

Chapter Twenty-Two

The chilling water from her long hair hid her tears as Ilona clasped Garth to her breast and began to wipe away the sweat from his fevered brow. He was shaking—far beyond shivering. The cold and exhaustion, coupled with an apparent lack of food, had driven him into a semi-conscious delirium in which he seemed unable to recognize her.

"Aiiii . . . he is going to die," she wailed to herself as she stoked the remains of his fire into a decent blaze, then dragged Garth as close to it as she dared. Even that brief interaction seemed too much for him, and he was unconscious again when she slipped back into the icy water and disappeared beneath the mist.

This time she emerged from the treacherous waters on René's side of the river and surfaced to find the small voyageur pacing impatiently, clearly distraught at having watched her dive naked into the surging waters and then disappear.

He wrapped her in a blanket while she briefly explained the situation, then insisted that he must try to swim through the waterfall and help to rescue his friend. Twice he tried, and then had to give up. He was simply not a strong enough swimmer to fight the writhing currents beneath the curtain of water that poured more than a hundred feet from the crest.

After his second attempt nearly drowned him, Ilona managed to convince René that he would be of more help by providing them with fresh meat, which she thought necessary to rebuild

Garth's strength so that maybe . . . maybe . . . she could assist him to swim out.

"It will be difficult for him, I think," she said. "His ankle is badly hurt, maybe broken, and I think his back is also hurt. I have already looked, and I could find no other way in or out of the place that is under the waterfall. We will have to swim, and to do that he will need food and warmth and some time to recover his strength. And me."

Her own return to the cavern beneath the falls nearly drowned her. She couldn't find the right current patterns at first and was hampered by René's parfleche, the buckskin bag he'd used to carry pemmican, and the blanket he had tied around her. She kept being repulsed by the strength of the waters. It took three tries before she emerged inside the water cave, where she found Garth seemingly no worse, but also unimproved.

She had no choice but to neglect him long enough to dry herself off by the fire. The cold, for her, threatened to be a worse enemy than the rushing waters. Untended, she knew only too well, it would kill them both. Then she examined Garth, noting the grotesquely swollen ankle and the cuts and bruises all over him from Savard's assault and from the river's adding to it.

She also took the time to explore the cavern more closely but had to accept disappointment. It looked like there might be a way out from one side of the waterfall during late summer's lower water flow, but now . . . no hope at all.

So she made one more journey through the currents, this time returning more easily and bringing René's tea-pail and more pemmican. The pemmican was good quality, but she would have preferred fresh, hot meat.

For the next four days she never left Garth's side except to swim quickly outside to see if René had found meat. Which he had—a fat young moose calf on the second day. She kept Garth wrapped in the blanket and kept the fire going steadily. But it was her own healthy young body she used to warm him when he shook with chills, and she cried out in delight when his fever broke and he looked at her with an expression approaching recognition.

"My God, I must be dreaming," he whispered before she shushed him with one finger. Then she cradled his head upon her lap and patiently spooned a soupy stew into him until he groaned and once again fell into sleep.

The following few days, despite the pain of his throbbing ankle, were days of pure delight for Garth. Ilona spent virtually every waking moment with him, not in any shy silence, but as a delightful, sparkling young girl, vivid with laughter at his humor and gently caring for his needs.

All of his needs. They were as young lovers on a deserted island, filled with hope and joy in each other's presence and ostensibly without a care in the entire world. They dined on thick steaks from the moose René had killed, and then—miracle of miracles—on the fat trout René caught in the rapids below the falls.

They rested, and healed, and learned about each other, adjusting to each other's gestures and feelings, and touch. Ilona was a maiden, but her Indian upbringing had prepared her for what was involved in all that. Garth was already fluent in the physical aspects but had never before been with a woman he loved, or thought he loved, and he was unprepared for many of the nuances in that.

Only once did the aura of enchantment falter, and that but briefly. When Garth tried to question Ilona about her time with Savard, she gently evaded his questions, slowly slipping into her native shell of impassiveness whenever he continued with his queries. It would serve no purpose, she knew, for her lover to even think about her travails at the hands of the giant half-breed, and even though she had escaped Savard with her maidenhood intact, she doubted Garth's ability to recognize that, or the gift of her innocence she had given him with that first coupling beneath the surging, singing waterfall.

On one wet trip through the falling curtain of the water, she brought her own clothing, such as it was, and spent some of their time together making repairs to their smoke-tanned garments. Daily, Garth's health and strength improved, until they could no longer delay the inevitable.

And even then it was Ilona—or so she made it seem—who made the decision. Still damp with perspiration from their early-morning lovemaking, she announced that it was time to go.

"The river has been going down for days . . . you can see it," she said. "But at this time of year there will be storms in the mountains, and it would take only one such storm to make it so we can't get out of here for half a moon or more."

Slipping into the pool, she ducked beneath the waterfall and returned after some time with a coil of rawhide rope and a heavy length of green poplar. Gathering the rope with this weight attached, she crept to the edge of the cavern and flipped the poplar chunk out to where she hoped René might catch it. It took the old voyageur three tries, but Garth could see how the plan might unfold.

Not entirely trusting his untested strength, Ilona knotted the rope around his wrist, then kissed him briefly on the cheek and slid away into the pool with the agility and grace of an oversized otter, leaving him to wait, alone, on the slippery ledge.

Some minutes later Garth felt the line tense. As planned, he slid himself off the ledge and into the roiling waters that had nearly killed him. He had time for only one quick breath before he felt himself being drawn down and against the strain of the rope. He knew old René and Ilona were braced amid the rocks outside, trying to use their bodies as the lever on which Garth could best the currents beneath the waterfall's curtain, but he didn't have Ilona's studied knowledge of the currents he faced.

He felt a moment of panic, then a piercing stab of pain in his ankle as it slammed into a submerged rock. Then he found himself free of the undertow and rising for a much-needed breath of fresh air outside the smashing curtain of the falls.

Peering through pain-dimmed eyes, he could see his two rescuers, Ilona helping René to drag him over to the flat shelf of rock on which they stood. Atop the riverbank, reached only with both Ilona and René dragging and pushing him with all their strength, he found that René had a good fire going and a steaming stewpot ready for them.

Then he watched through an unexpected sleepiness as Ilona used wet rawhide and stout sticks to create a proper splint for his ankle. The buckskin bindings from the cavern had never fully dried and had done little to properly support the break, but the way she created this splint it would dry iron-hard within hours as he rested by the fire and stay that way if they could keep it dry.

There was minimal pain once she had the ankle properly aligned, and Garth was only half awake when she left him and returned to their cavern to gather the rest of their belongings. Not a lot had been abandoned, but the tea pail was too valuable to leave behind.

They rested the day and night at their camp by the waterfall, with Garth and René in animated discussion about what they should do next. Garth was all for pursuing Savard, but the elderly voyageur was equally adamant in his decision to return to the Iroquois encampment and then back to Rocky Mountain House.

"*Mon Dieu,* I have followed that bastard half a day into the mountains while I hunt meat for you," he growled. "He is gone west, probably over the mountains, and that is not where we should even think of going. We have only one horse, and not a very sound one, at that. It would be hard enough for the poor beast to carry you back down the river and then south to the big river, the Saskatchewan, without us traipsing into the mountains on some wild goose chase. Me, I think Savard must be dead or dying. There is nobody out there to help him, and he lost much blood when the little Climbing Woman, she stuck the knife in his guts. Forget him, my friend. We go south, and we go slowly, since you are not as strong as you think. If we are very lucky, we might make it back to our *patron* before he decides to return downriver and back to the company headquarters in the east."

Garth's futile arguments were ignored. In the morning, they bundled him in blankets and robes, loaded him on René's pony, and headed off along the Kakwa to where old Henri Wanyandie and his people were breaking up their own winter camp and readying for the southward hunting trip into buffalo country.

It was a far easier trip downstream, overall, than either Garth or René had experienced when they'd gone upstream along the Kakwa. Warm spring winds had eaten the worst of the snow and dried the trail in most places. The south fork crossing was still high enough to challenge the short-legged pony, but with René's urging he crossed without dumping Garth into the icy current.

The deaths of Elise and Monique had left their mark on the faces of the Wanyandie family, but they greeted Garth as if he had not been involved. He was carried into a vacant cabin and put to bed. The band's medicine man, skilled in such matters, was brought to check Garth's ankle and other injuries, and several of the younger girls were enlisted to help Ilona care for him during the few days before departure.

Ilona put her foot down. No one but her, she declared in strong but dignified tones, would care for Garth. She had saved him from the *pawastik*, the falling water, and she could care for him adequately now, she said.

Old René took no part in the discussion, being more intent upon readying them for departure with the Iroquois band when it headed off to the south. With help from young Daniel Wanyandie, he sought out a strong but relatively placid mare to carry Garth, then found a spanking, high-spirited buckskin for Ilona and a shaggy roan packhorse for their gear.

"We must have horses that don't stand out too much," he told Garth that evening. "We can only travel a short way with these Iroquois. The rest we must do alone, and there will be other Indians to worry about; Sleeping Elk, for sure, and maybe even the Blackfoot. Who knows? They may all be at war by now."

Chapter Twenty-Three

Garth, Ilona, and René traveled a week with the Iroquois, southeast to Daniel Flats, then upstream on the Muskeg River and overland to the Rock Lake junction of the trails. From there, said old Henri, his people would go southeast to seek the buffalo.

"We do not go very far out onto the plains. It is too far, and we have too many enemies there," he said. "But there are herds of the buffalo of the woods, and these we shall find down along the flats of the Athabasca or maybe a bit north on the Wildhay.

"You must go south and west, to avoid the people of Sleeping Elk. They are moving ahead of us toward the Athabasca, according to the signs, which is good for you but maybe not so good for us. There is a trail south from here along what we call Snake Indian River. It passes west of the Medicine Springs and then south through the mountains to the start of the big river. I think that is the one you call the Saskatchewan, but I am not sure."

There was much emotion in the partings, particularly on the part of Ilona, who had become as a daughter to the old chief. René, also, did not leave the camp dry eyed. His winter with the widow Red Willow had left her heavy with child, and he was half-tempted, he admitted, to take her south with them.

"If it was only the one *bébé*, I would not mind so much," he said, "but she has the other three children, too. It would not be right to separate them from their people. If we were both younger . . . maybe."

So he kissed the woman fondly, then kicked his horse away to join Garth and Ilona, who were already a quarter-mile down the trail to Snake Indian River.

Three days later they reached the high, narrow lake that René said he thought was the beginning of the Athabasca. And there they found pony tracks in the sand . . . tracks that raised the hackles on the back of Garth's neck and caused René to cease his softly-sung litany of brash river songs.

"*Sacré!* It is Savard, or at least his horses. I know these tracks anywhere, even in my sleep," René growled. "Can nothing kill that devil? Truly, he is like *le Carcajou*, the devil wolverine."

The tracks were so obvious, Garth would have recognized them even without René's expertise as a tracker and woodsman. He said nothing but rode with increased caution and checked his firearm's priming every few minutes despite René's insistence they were days behind their enemy.

Ilona glanced at the tracks and did her best to conceal the instinctive shudder of fear and distaste she felt.

Several miles past the western point of the lake, they crossed the river to rest near a cold sulfur spring that poured from the mountainside and could be smelled half a mile away.

When they started off again, René noticed Savard's tracks had disappeared. The disclosure caused immediate consternation for René. He cursed and roughly turned his pony back so he could recheck the trail. "We must know where that bastard is going," he muttered.

He caught up with Garth and Ilona a few miles further along, noticeably relieved and happy to report that their nemesis apparently had turned east from the springs, along the southern shore of the lake.

"Just as well," said Garth, still unable to walk properly for any distance, although healing fast in the improvised rawhide cast. He balked at René's refusal to follow Savard but had to admit he would be of little use in a fight.

"And I want to fight the bastard myself," he growled as they lounged beside their small fire that night. "I can whip him, given a fair start. He's really just a big, clumsy bear, all muscle and no brains."

"Such confidence is reassuring, but maybe a little foolhardy," René responded. "You must remember you have already had a chance at him, and look where that got you . . . trying to shoot the rapids without even a canoe."

Even Ilona laughed at the voyageur's inept joke, but Garth wasn't amused. "He was lucky, that's all. If my foot hadn't slipped, it would have been him floating down the river. I sort of wish it had been. By now he'd be squatting under that waterfall and eating the last of his buckskins."

"And if it was not for the shy one, here," René said, nodding toward Ilona, "it would still be you there." René gave an enigmatic shrug. "Count your blessings before you curse someone else, even Savard."

It was difficult for the old man to note who blushed the most at his comments, Garth or the lovely Ilona. He had noticed the way the two rode closely together during a part of each day, always when the trail was clear enough so Garth's vigilance wasn't imperative for their safety. Clearly, they both assumed he wouldn't notice their feelings, but to a man of René's experience and years, they might as well have shouted it from the nearest mountain crest . . . and there were plenty of those.

They followed the trail southeast to Maligne Lake, then turned more southward until they struck the Brazeau downstream from the lake it was named for. In camp that night, René and Garth discussed the relative merits of heading further south to Sunset Pass and the trail down the Cline to the

Saskatchewan, or following the Brazeau down to hit the big river somewhere near the trading post known as Northwest House. Chief among their concerns were the likely summer movements of the Sunchild Cree led by the crippled and unpredictable Small Bear.

They quickly agreed that the mountain Blackfoot of Garth's early captivity would have gone east to the buffalo along the Red Deer River, far to the south of them, but they couldn't agree about the possible movements of the Sunchild Cree. Garth felt certain they would have crossed the Saskatchewan to hunt along the Medicine River or the headwaters of the Battle, but René said it might yet be too early in the season, and the Cree might well have lingered along the Brazeau.

He won the argument, even though they found out the next day he was as wrong as Garth. The Cree were not downstream on the Brazeau but headed up into the mountains towards Sunwapta Pass.

Garth and René watched in silence as the entire Sunchild band crossed the river below their hiding place on a bluff high above. The band took the trail that would traverse the slope not half a mile below the bluff. The band headed for the same crossing Garth and René had headed out early to scout, leaving Ilona to clean up the camp and pack the spare pony.

"Where the hell are they going?" Garth whispered after the lengthy brigade of mounted warriors, laden travois ponies, and yapping dogs had moved past. "I don't think that's Small Bear's outfit . . . I didn't see him. But some of the others look familiar."

"It is Small Bear's band," René whispered in reply, not bothering to look at his companion because he was too focused on the last of the Indian procession. "But now I'm thinking somebody else is leading them. Maybe Painted Horse. Aha . . . that is what has happened. Small Bear has died, and they are taking him to the mountain for a funeral ceremony. Damn! I am *très* glad we do not have to ride downwind of them. I bet you that Small Bear has been dead for days, maybe even a week, and by the time they reach their burial ground he will smell high enough to draw every grizzly bear in the country."

René fell silent as the Indians moved over a low ridge and out of sight, then turned quickly away, drawing Garth with him.

"Now let us go quickly and collect the little Climbing Woman and get moving. If we are lucky, we can cross their tracks and lose our trail in theirs. Sooner or later, some of their hunters will be along, and if one picks up our trail, we will really be in trouble."

Garth, René, and Ilona spent valuable time crossing the Indians' trail in such a way as to conceal their own movements, turning back to the ford only after various deceptive moves by René. Their four horses were right in the middle of the ford when a strange Indian rode out into the stream from the south, head down and watching only his own pony's footing. He looked up to find René making the universal peace sign and replied to it before kneeing his pony toward them.

Garth held back and casually kept his rifle aimed at the Indian as the stranger and René drew abreast in the shallows of the ford.

He missed a good deal of the conversation, which was a jumble of sign language and bastard Cree, but he picked up enough to recognize that René had been right, and Small Bear was indeed dead and being taken to the band's sacred burial ground. The strange warrior showed no sign of hostility, but Garth kept his rifle casually on the man until the crossing was complete and both parties had reached the relatively safety of the timber.

Safely ashore, the strange warrior kicked his pony to a run, crouched low over its back and weaving a zigzag path through the underbrush. Garth was tempted to try a snap shot, but René interrupted him.

"Never mind, my friend. Instead, let us worry about getting a long way from this place before that one comes back with friends. With the funeral planned, they would not chase us too far, I think, but I would not like to tempt them. If we are *très* lucky, he will get nobody interested in chasing us until the ceremonies are over."

Pushing their horses, they reached Sunset Pass by early afternoon, and by dark, after several deceptive attempts by René—"probably a waste of time; these warriors would be better at tracking than an old man like me"—they were nearing the mouth of Coral Creek where it joined with the Cline. There was a good, logical campsite there and no sign of pursuit, but René's instincts were speaking to him, and he ordered a dry and fireless camp well away from the stream.

René's precautions gave them a half-mile start on the seven young warriors who picked up their trail just before dawn and came whooping down on the campsite by the creek mouth.

Ilona had finished loading the pack pony, and Garth and René were mounting up when they heard the shrill war cries and the unnerving, abrupt silence that followed as the Indians realized their mistake.

Spurring up a narrow ridge trail beside the creek, René slowed only long enough to mutter a brief, "I told you so!" as Garth and Ilona sped past him. Then he took seemingly casual aim at the first Indian to reach the foot of the incline and dropped him with a single shot.

The remaining half dozen screeched around in the bush for a while, building up their nerve for an assault on the hill. When Garth shot the leader of that attempt and René killed the second-place horse, the youthful warriors abandoned the chase.

"Not Small Bear's people," René said as the trio hurried to put more distance between themselves and the possibility of more hostilities. "Blackfoot, I think. Maybe out looking for trouble, but there are too many Indians in the area to suit me."

Reaching the Bighorn, the trio turned slightly north to Garth's old hiding place near the Crescent Falls. This small nook was crowded by the four horses, but, with Blackfoot on the prowl, René decided safety was the primary consideration and again demanded a quiet, fireless camp.

Recurring close calls with small, roving bands of hostiles veered them considerably north of their planned route, and it was the end of the sixth day before they dropped down off a ridge to find themselves on the most southerly corner of the Baptiste River.

"One more day, maybe two at the most, and we should be home," René said, now prepared to allow a camp complete with water and warm food. "I make it forty-two days since we left the Kakwa; not bad considering all the damned Indians we have to avoid, *non*?"

Garth, equally jubilant about the success of their journey, proposed a hearty toast of river water to mark the occasion, but Ilona remained pensively quiet despite the excitement of her companions.

For once, it was Garth who noticed the girl's somber mood. His own happiness dimmed as he sat quietly watching her across the smoldering fire, noting with pleasure the lovely contours of her face and the flowing sheaves of raven hair that framed it. Slipping quietly to his feet, he circled the blaze and squatted beside her, placing one arm around her shoulders.

"What's the matter, little one?" he asked. "Aren't you pleased to be so close to home? Or would you rather spend the rest of the summer riding the high trails with me?"

She cast him one startled glance, then leapt to her feet and sprang away into the darkness, but not before he saw a single tear start down her cheek. Garth had half turned to follow her when he was stopped by a low word from René.

"Let her go, you fool. Can you not see she wants to be alone? Damn, but you can be a stupid youngster sometimes."

"But what the hell did I do? Christ, all I did was put my arm around her. Can I do nothing right?"

The query brought only a baleful glance from René, so Garth squatted again by the fire, idly chewing on a piece of dry meat as he stared into the flames. After several minutes he glanced up to see the elderly voyageur looking not at him, but off into the darkness, and he remembered another piece of sage advice from his old friend.

"Never look into the night fire," old René had warned him long ago. "It blinds you when you look away then into the darkness, and it might mean your death if there is a Blackfoot scalping knife out there."

"But there's no Blackfoot out there tonight," Garth whispered to himself, though he turned away from the fire, chilled by the possibility. Moments later, Ilona strode back into camp. She rolled into her blankets without a word and curled up with her back to them.

It was as if her heavy mood brought inclement weather with it. Heavy rains the next day slowed their journey and dampened their excitement. They all rode slumped sodden in their saddles, and Garth was too miserable with the rain to note that Ilona spoke not a single word to him during the last stages of the journey.

When they arrived at Rocky Mountain House, Ilona sprang from her pony and scampered straight toward her father's lodge, but Garth hardly noticed in the excitement of their welcome. It seemed everyone had long since given them up for dead and now saw their miraculous return as a good excuse for a soiree.

David Thompson was away downriver, visiting at Boggy Hall, but most of the others were on hand: Grouard, Paul the clerk, old Pierre, and the various other members of the lengthy trading expedition.

Their arrival called for a celebration, said Grouard, and surely the factor would expect a tot of rum for all concerned, so it was out with the rum keg and the fiddles and a massive feast of roast goose and hump meat and venison roasts.

Garth ate until he could eat no more, while old René ate and drank and ate again until he stumbled into a corner and passed out on the floor. Garth helped carry him to their cabin, took one look at the other bunk, and promptly sprawled out for a twelve-hour nap.

CHAPTER TWENTY-FOUR

The plains and mountain tribes all knew various methods of promoting abortion. Ilona tried them all, but nothing worked.

On the fifth morning she'd stumbled from her cot with bile rising in her throat as she fled the cabin, old Jean-Paul took note of his daughter's condition and wished—not for the first time as he'd tried to raise a motherless daughter—that his wife was still alive. His beautiful wife, Grouse Wing, had died in the plague of '98, along with half the Stoney tribe they had been traveling with. The smallpox had bothered neither the child Ilona nor her aging father, but her mother had less resistance.

He had taken no other woman since her death, though at times he had felt, for Ilona's sake, that it might be a worthy idea. But Grouse Wing had borne him a dozen children in their twenty years together on the rivers and in the high mountain wilderness. He wanted no other woman; needed none. For a while, he had half expected his child-daughter to be a nuisance, but Ilona had grown up quickly, and at ten years of age was already keeping his camps almost as well as her mother had.

Nothing in their time together, however, had prepared him for the eventuality he now faced—a daughter heading for childbirth without a man in the picture. Or at least no man she would allow to be involved. Not in itself a terrible sin by Indian standards. It happened. But to a woman of Ilona's sensitivity . . .

"Daughter, it comes to me that you and I must have a talk," he said when she returned to the cabin's dingy interior, her lovely face pale and drawn from the effort of vomiting. "It is clear that you are with child, but you have no man that I can see. Ever since you returned here to our post, you have avoided young Cameron like he had fleas or something. Is he the father? And what has gone wrong between you? Or did he—"

"He does not know," she interrupted, "but, yes, he is the father, and no, he did not force me. It is just that—"

"Good. That saves me the trouble of having to cut out his heart. But you must know that soon you will not be able to hide your condition. Soon the whole post will know of it. So why not young Cameron? He cares for you; we both know that. Cares a great deal, I would say . . . he has risked his life for you several times, spent half a year trying to rescue you from that bastard Savard."

"He does, and he has always treated me properly," Ilona managed before shattering in a holocaust of tears.

It took old Jean-Paul an hour of pleading and comforting and threatening the girl before the entire story of her winter with the Iroquois came out in full detail, and with it, the source of her real problem—René!

"He rode away from the widow Red Willow, leaving her heavy with his child and with her other children still to care for," Ilona said bitterly. "And we both know that is the common way things are done here between the two peoples. Well, not for me! I will not be any man's leftover."

"*Mon Dieu,* my daughter, you must not confuse the actions of an old voyageur like René with how young Cameron feels about you and what is to come. You cannot know what is in the man's mind if you will not even talk to him," her father replied. "He is in love with you . . . even I can see that . . . and you with him, *non*? So what if you carry his woods colt? Is Cameron not enough of a man to accept what has happened? I do not think you give him enough credit."

But Ilona made the cut-off sign, and her eyes grew cold, and her aging father knew he must accept her judgment, as he had to accept it when she fled the cabin again to deal with her morning sickness.

Garth was too busy to do more than casually notice Ilona's avoidance of him and wonder at it. He and René had been appointed chief scouts for the post, and spent the majority of their days and nights on the trail, hunting game and keeping an eye peeled for signs of hostile Indians.

Of equal interest was the variety of activities obvious in the camp of the Hudson's Bay Company men at Acton. The rivalry between the Hudson's Bay Company and the North-West Company was always tenuous, brittle, and often fraught with violence. David Thompson, their *patron* and the factor at Rocky Mountain House, had begun his career with the Hudson's Bay Company but left it after thirteen years because the governor objected to his mapping and surveying activities. His subsequent sojourns with the Norwesters did little to resolve the rivalries.

Relations between the traders and staff at the Bay's Acton House and Thompson's Rocky Mountain House had deteriorated even without Savard's presence during the winter René and Garth had spent with the Iroquois on the Kakwa, the Porcupine River, and tensions were near the breaking point.

Henry Papien, noted among the Norwesters as a capable and rough fighting man, staggered into the post one night with one eye missing, an ear half torn from his head, and a variety of cuts and bruises that suggested he might have lost an argument with a hungry bear.

"Bear, hell! It was company men of the Bay," he cursed while having his wounds attended. "I went over to the Cree camp for a little fun with a squaw, and on the way back . . . well . . . I wasn't paying much attention to the trail. By God, three of them jumped me, and the next thing I know I am lying there half dead. But my mark is on one of them, for sure, and another, I kick him so hard in the balls he won't piss for a month, him."

When asked who they were, he said, "How the hell would I know that? It was pitch black there in the night. You couldn't see the end of your nose, and before the fight was hardly started I had lost one eye, and the other was swelling shut."

To make matters worse, it was obvious Thompson's post was being undercut in dealings with the Indians in a deliberate attempt to promote open hostility to the North-West Company's trade. And it was working.

Summer furs were seldom worth bothering with, but the number of drunken natives hanging around Acton House made it obvious the Bay people were trading freely with their rum. Several members of the mountain Blackfoot, formerly led by Three Bears, were regular visitors at both posts, getting half drunk at Acton House and then pounding on the gates of Rocky Mountain House with demands for more of the trade rum. Their leader now was the old chief's second son, *Mahekun*, the Wolf, and he was even meaner towards the whites than Three Bears and Walking Dog ever had been.

Garth and René were trailing a group of young Blackfoot north along the Clearwater one morning when the elderly voyageur stopped his pony with a vitriolic curse and leapt to the ground in a gesture that belied his age.

"Look at this, my young friend," he hissed. "Aaaiii . . . there will be blood along the Saskatchewan now, for sure. That son-of-a-bitch Savard is back, or else his ghost, and those of his ponies. Look at these tracks, and tell me I am wrong."

Garth crouched beside his friend and felt his stomach knot at the sight. The tracks were undeniably those of the ponies Savard had been using when they last saw his spoor by the cold sulfur spring to the north, and from the depth of the hoof prints on *this* ground, one of the ponies was being ridden by someone as heavy as Savard. It was too much of a coincidence to ignore.

"Come! We must go now to the post," René said. "It is only a day's ride if we hurry, and, God knows, we might be too late even then. It is no wonder these damned Blackfoot have been so much trouble, if Savard has been stirring them up."

Ignoring the tracks they had been following, or the vague possibility of riding into an ambush, they kicked their ponies to full gallop and headed north to the river. René rode with only the thought of averting a trade war, but Garth found thoughts of Ilona growing incessantly in his head as they thundered down the narrow canyon trail along the Clearwater.

Fully recovered from his ordeals of the spring, he now felt confident he could deal with Savard man to man, although he worried he mightn't have time to arrange such a showdown soon enough to avert bloody warfare all along the Saskatchewan. But when they thundered into the post late that night, they found no evidence of trouble to come. René headed immediately to the factor's cabin to alert David Thompson, if the factor was back from Boggy Hall, while Garth put away the horses and stowed their gear.

Then, with misgivings about not immediately seeking out Ilona and her father, he began a cautious scout around the perimeter of the post. All was quiet, particularly and unusually so, he noticed, within the palisades of neighboring Acton House. Late as it was, he thought, there should have been *some* activity there. He was slinking past the adjacent camp of the free trappers, hoping for a better approach to the back edge of the Acton House compound, when he spotted a shadowy movement in the timber to his right.

He stopped, knife drawn and ready, and watched a shrouded figure moving parallel to his own path.

Garth leapt forward toward the figure, only to halt in amazement as the moonlight revealed the face of Ilona, who had obviously known all along who he was and where he was.

"My God, woman, you might have been killed. Don't you know any better than to follow a man around like this in the night?"

"I have come to warn you that Savard has returned," she said in a hushed voice. "I saw him. He is down at the end of the camp now, plotting with some of the free trappers and most of the men from the Bay post. They are going to overrun your post first thing in the morning, I think."

"Surely things aren't that bad between the companies," Garth objected. "There is competition, of course, but—"

"It is true. The Blackfoot of *Mahekun* are waiting at the mouth of the Clearwater, and they will attack once it is going well, to make it look like an Indian massacre. All of your people, and any who do not join Savard, are to be killed."

Garth didn't hesitate. "I'm going there now," he said. "I'll stop Savard at the free traders' camp . . . somehow . . . even if I have to kill him. You must go back to our post and rouse René and the others. But tell René not to come there. Tell him he must defend Rocky Mountain House at all cost."

Pulling her against him in a sudden gesture, Garth kissed her quickly, whispered, "I love you," and slid away into the darkness, leaving Ilona to stand there a moment, stunned by his revelation, before she turned and sped back toward the Norwesters' post to rouse René and those loyal to the factor.

CHAPTER TWENTY-FIVE

There were perhaps fifty men present when Garth snuck up on the free trappers' gathering, and for such a large group of such rugged individualists, they were amazingly quiet, he thought.

Only the bull voice of Louis Savard was obvious, dominating the scene and overriding the few objections that faltered forth from others. Virtually all of the free trappers had—in past times—traded with both the major companies, and everyone present knew David Thompson, but the free trappers were seldom united on anything, and the men of Acton House who were present formed a solid block of antagonism.

"By damn, I am Louis Savard. You all know me, and you know I used to lead these men of the Bay," Savard shouted, prowling round the fire as if to speak to everyone individually. And lying, although nobody raised the issue. After his assault on the Acton House factor the year before, he did not—technically—lead the Bay employees at all. But he spoke well, and his imposing presence was no hindrance. "The woods are not wide enough for us and the Norwesters too. They must be driven from the Saskatchewan, and you all know why. They cheat the Indians, and we get blamed for it."

More lies, thought Garth, but not easy to dispute.

Savard promised to lead the revolt he was fomenting. "And, yes, protect you too from the Blackfoot as well," he said. "*Mahekun*, the Wolf, waits at the mouth of the Clearwater. He will finish what we begin, and, when it is all over, Thompson will return from Boggy Hall to find only an Indian massacre, his post burned, and no chance to rebuild. The Norwesters must leave this land while there are still beaver enough for the Bay company, and for you, the free trappers and traders who have opened up this country. Do you want to give it all away?"

Garth could sense uncertainty within the listening group, and he knew any action he might take had best be done soon, before Savard whipped everyone into a senseless mob and aimed them at the unsuspecting men of Rocky Mountain House.

As Savard paused for breath between his rants, Garth sprang into the circle of firelight, surprising many of the men gathered there and—hopefully—surprising Savard.

"What is all this shit?" Garth bellowed. "You want to be led by this poseur Savard?" He faced his nemesis directly, one hand always close to the knife in his belt. "You couldn't lead a moose to its wallow, you overstuffed pig. Why don't you tell them what a wonderful leader you were to the Cardinal brothers? Go on: tell them who killed Elzear and Lucien."

He didn't give Savard time to reply before flinging his words at the big man in a volley of abuse. "Would you kill all these men, too, after they'd done your filthy work?" he asked and was pleased to see at least some of the free traders paying attention.

"I will kill you, Cameron," Savard hissed, his voice so low only those nearest could hear him. "And then I will take that woman of yours and—"

"And what?" Garth knew he must control the fight or lose it. He *had* to keep the bigger man off balance, so full of rage he couldn't think straight. "Your killing time is done, Savard, and this time I will wear your scalp on my belt until I can't stand the stink of it any longer. Come on, what are you afraid of? Throw down your rifle, and bring out your toad-sticker. We'll finish this right here and now and show these pissants how little it takes for a real man to show you up."

Garth almost thought he'd not gone far enough to provoke Savard into a fight with knives and fists, rather than guns, but the huge half-breed handed his rifle to the man nearest him and erupted in a roar of defiance as he leapt toward Garth with his knife held low and deadly.

Garth had just enough time to draw his own knife, and then the two men merged in a blur of movement, circling the fire like wreaths of smoke, their blades gleaming in the firelight. Neither man touched the other, although their knives struck sparks with virtually every stroke, and the crowd of watchers spread out to give them room to fight.

Garth, along with Savant, drew off to seek a new approach, circling slowly beside the fire as they measured each other in search of an opening, a perceived weakness. Both were breathing heavily. Garth heard the spectators began to clap and chant, striving to bring the contest back into action again.

Savard's patience broke first. He sprang from a half crouch to land in the middle of the flames, blade streaking toward Garth's partially-exposed groin. Garth, twisting to avoid the stroke, missed his guard and balance, and nearly stumbled into the crowding circle of watchers.

He had momentary glimpses of men gathered around the outskirts of the firelight: René, little Paul, and the Norwesters from his own camp. Distracted, he nearly got cut again before he dove back into the fray, slashing back and forth to drive Savard into a defensive position and, incidentally, inflict a slight gash on the bigger man's arm.

Again, they circled the fire like two large hunting cats, neither able to manage a critical thrust. Garth knew it would take only a single misstep to change the odds. Obviously, Savard knew it, too.

Breathing faster, Garth noted with some satisfaction that his larger opponent seemed to be running short of wind. Garth smiled at the thought, then slipped on a piece of firewood and went almost to his knees to evade Savard's slashing attack. A kick from the big man's moccasined foot sent Garth back into the crowd of onlookers, and he felt a harsh fist drive into his kidneys, thrusting him toward Savard and his weapon. Garth managed a quick thrust with his left foot that drove Savard backwards but caused Garth to fall flat and almost in the flames.

Savard, quick as a diving beaver, hurled himself at Garth, driving his wicked knife at Garth's chest, but Garth whipped his torso around sideways, and Savard's knife hand drove deep into the glowing coals. He howled and released his blade as he struggled to regain his feet.

Garth, sensing rather than hearing the growls of disapproval from the Bay company spectators, threw his own knife to the ground behind him and leapt forward to grapple hand to hand with Savard. In such combat, he knew, the bigger man's strength would be a clear advantage, but Garth had no time to think about that. He grasped Savard's rising left arm and attempted to throw him backward into the flames without being dragged in himself.

The ruse worked, and Garth backed off as Savard came out of the fire with both hands swinging in an attempt to grasp Garth's arms or clothing or hair. Garth took his chance and used his boxing skills to drive three swift blows to Savard's stomach and face.

One blow opened a cut on the big man's cheekbone while another split the skin over one eye.

Three times Garth struck Savard mightily on the chin, but the blows were shielded by the giant's bushy beard, which also protected his throat. He was staggered but didn't slow down enough for Garth to land a decisive punch.

Worse, the effort was telling upon Garth's stamina, and each blow he struck made him more vulnerable to his opponent's grasping rushes. He and Savant were visibly panting, silent now in their battle.

Garth had renewed hope he could defeat the giant, but then someone tripped him from behind, and he felt Savard's weight smash down onto him. Twisting one thigh, he managed to protect his groin from the knee that crunched downward, but he couldn't entirely avoid the slashing thumb that scraped past his ear.

Now it was Savard's type of fighting, and he took every opportunity to use outright strength to drag Garth into the circle of his massive arms. Garth knew he was weakening and found himself slowly being drawn into a deadly bear hug that might well mean the end of the fight. Ducking his head to protect his throat, he managed to throw it backwards and up to smash into Savard's face, crushing the man's already damaged nose. Savard roared with anguish and released the pressure enough so that Garth could fight free.

Savard reached blindly toward him, blood streaming from smashed lips and nostrils. Garth seized the outstretched wrist, twisted Savard over his shoulder, and flung him clear across the fire pit and into the crowd.

Staggering to hold onto his own balance, Garth turned then to hear a rumble of disapproval from the onlookers. He looked up to see Savard rising to his knees, rifle in hand and swinging it to aim at Garth.

Garth was poised to throw himself to one side when a tawny shape crossed his vision as Ilona flung herself through the air to knock aside the rifle even as it discharged in a gout of flame and smoke.

As Garth launched himself across the fire pit toward Savard, he saw the burly woods boss swing the rifle butt, smashing it into Ilona's stomach and driving her to a gasping heap beside the scattered, dying fire.

211

CHAPTER TWENTY-SIX

Garth had no memory of finishing the fight, but they told him later it didn't take him long.

"*Mon Dieu,* I never have seen a man so angry," René told him. "You leap across the fire and kick him in the throat, then you drag him into the fire by his hair and stomp his face in the coals, and then, by gar, if you don't hold him by the beard and kick him in the balls five, maybe ten times. I think myself maybe he'd be dead already by then, but it is not enough for you. Such a fight! Three hundred pounds, he must weigh, and you pick him up like *le bébé,* and then you pound his head against a tree until there is nothing left to scalp.

"I tell you, these Hudson Bay men they get sick when they see that. I'm thinking they don't bother us now for a long time. We mention your name now, and they turn green with fear."

Exhaustion had ended the fight for Garth. After pounding Savard against the tree trunk, he had dropped the man's body by the flames and then collapsed beside it, his stomach heaving even as he lost consciousness.

René told him later about the minor skirmish that drove the Wolf's Blackfoot into a total rout. "You missed that little fight," René said, "but it was not so much."

Garth was up and about the next day, albeit somewhat unsteady on his feet, but it was two days after that before he was allowed to visit Ilona, pale as death itself on a cot in her father's lodge.

"You must be careful not to upset her," her father warned him in no uncertain terms. "She has suffer . . . what you call it? . . . a miscarriage. She lost a lot of blood and nearly died. Maybe will die yet if you do not treat her gently, but I think she will want to see you."

Ilona's face was a ghostly color, and her slender hand trembled as Garth lifted it to his lips and knelt by her bedside, but her eyes were alive, and he fancied they were strong with the love he hoped was reflected from his own.

When his tears came, he didn't know what to say or how to say anything at all. He could only reach out with clumsy fingers and try to brush them away as they spilled downward to mingle with Ilona's own tears.

Nonetheless, the words spilled from him as readily as did his tears—words of love, of respect, and of devotion. And of hope.

There would be other children, he told her, hopefully many of them, and there would be a wedding, as well. She must recover from her injuries so that when this trading season ended, they could both head down the mighty Saskatchewan to find a minister of the cloth or a black-robed priest, as her own parents had done when that opportunity presented itself.

And in the meantime, they would make do with marriage *à la façon du pays*—after the fashion of the country. So long as they had each other, it would suffice.

ABOUT THE AUTHOR

G. K. Aalborg is a native of north and western Alberta and grew up on tales of the early fur trade along the North Saskatchewan. As a journalist, he studied and wrote about the area's fur trade history and heritage and the involvement of the native peoples in that heritage.

He has fished for rainbow trout in the waters below Kakwa Falls and ridden many of the trails mentioned in this story.

He is also the author of *The Horse Tamer's Challenge* (Five Star: 2009) and more than two dozen other novels of mystery and romance.

For more info visit www.gordonaalborg.com.

The employees of Five Star Publishing hope you have enjoyed this book.

Our Five Star novels explore little-known chapters from America's history, stories told from unique perspectives that will entertain a broad range of readers.

Other Five Star books are available at your local library, bookstore, all major book distributors, and directly from Five Star/Gale.

Connect with Five Star Publishing

Visit us on Facebook:
https://www.facebook.com/FiveStarCengage

Email:
FiveStar@cengage.com

For information about titles and placing orders:
(800) 223-1244
gale.orders@cengage.com

To share your comments, write to us:
Five Star Publishing
Attn: Publisher
10 Water St., Suite 310
Waterville, ME 04901